PUFFIN BOOKS
Editor: Kaye Webb

YOURS EVER, SAM PIG

There have been many pigs, and some lovable
ones among them, but there is only one Sam
Pig. Whether he is simply taking a moonlight
stroll, talking over the gate to old Sally the
Mare, going to the village fête with Sister Ann
or watching Jack-in-the-Green dance on
Mayday, something mysterious or magical or
funny is bound to happen to him or his friends.

Boggarts spring up; bulls rage and gates sing
lullabies; wishes are granted and dreams come
true. There are squabbles with Brothers Bill
and Tom, expeditions with Ann, yarns with
old Sally and always Brock the Badger to keep
a wise and kindly eye over all.

Lovers of Sam Pig and Alison Uttley's
entrancing rural world, will welcome this
second Puffin collection of stories about him
(the first was *Adventures of Sam Pig*). All ages
can delight in it; six to nines may be
particularly charmed.

Alison Uttley

Yours Ever, Sam Pig

with drawings by A. E. Kennedy

Puffin Books
in association with Faber & Faber

Puffin Books,
Penguin Books Ltd,
Harmondsworth, Middlesex, England
Penguin Books,
625 Madison Avenue, New York, New York 10022, U.S.A.
Penguin Books Australia Ltd,
Ringwood, Victoria, Australia
Penguin Books Canada Ltd,
41 Steelcase Road West, Markham, Ontario, Canada
Penguin Books (N.Z.) Ltd,
182–190 Wairau Road, Auckland 10, New Zealand

First published by Faber & Faber 1951

Published in Puffin Books 1977

Copyright © Alison Uttley, 1951
Illustrations copyright © Faber & Faber 1951

Made and printed in Great Britain by
Hazell Watson & Viney Ltd,
Aylesbury, Bucks
Set in Linotype Baskerville

Contents

Sam Pig Writes a Letter

One day Sam Pig sat on the wall talking to Sally the Mare. The postman went up the lane with the letters and Sam and Sally looked at him through the branches of a tree. The postman didn't see the two pairs of eyes watching him, Sally's brown eyes and Sam's blue ones, for he was arranging a bundle of letters in his hands.

'Letters are nice things,' remarked Sam. 'I've never seen one, not really close. Not a true letter.'

'A pity you can't write, Sam,' said Sally. 'You've been to school and you can't even write a letter.'

'Only one day, Sally. I only went to school one day,' protested Sam.

'Surely it doesn't take more than a day to learn to write a letter?' asked Sally, staring at Sam. 'The postman carries heaps of letters in that bag, all written by somebodies, such as you and me.'

'How do you know?' asked Sam, twisting round on the wall and looking at the distant postman. He hitched his bag on his back and strode forward towards the farmhouse across the fields. In that bag were many letters.

'I've seen them, Sam. I've seen him give a few to Farmer Greensleeves, and he takes a package out of the bag, tied up with string, and looks through them.

' "No more today, Mister Greensleeves," says he.

' "Thank goodness for that. All bills," says Mister Greensleeves. "I wish you would bring me a nice letter with money in it, and not all these." '

'So the Farmer doesn't like his letters!' cried Sam. 'I thought letters were very nice things, like apples and cakes.'

'Some are nice and some are nasty,' said Sally, slowly. 'I often hear my master and mistress talking about letters. Now at Christmas they get very nice letters, and at birthdays and other times. Molly the dairymaid always gives a little cry of joy when she gets a letter. She hides it under her apron and reads it in the stable or the cowhouse. I've seen her. Then she kisses it. Yes, she always gets nice letters.'

Sam was much impressed by all this information.

'Sally, I might try to write one,' said he. 'I know my alphabet:

A is for Ann,
B is for Brock,
C is for Cabbage and
D is for Dock.'

'Of course you can do it,' said Sally, cheerfully. 'You wrote a Valentine for me once. You could write a letter, as good as anybody's. You're too modest, Sam.'

Sam puffed out his chest and put his hands in his pockets and thought about it. 'It would show them,' he murmured, darkly. 'It would show them what I can do if I try.'

'Of course you'll want a pen and ink and paper,' observed Sally, thoughtfully.

'I usually write with sticks and stones, and the ground is my paper, unless I write on a tree,' confessed Sam.

'A real letter to be carried by our postman must be written on paper,' said Sally, firmly. 'No postman will take bits of tree bark, or scraps of wood. It's going to be hard, Sam, but you can do it.'

'I never thought of all those things,' said Sam. 'But I used some ink once upon a time when I went to the Big House. I got in the library, through a glass door, and I climbed up to the desk where there was paper and ink. I didn't use a pen, Sally, for I hadn't been to school then. I used my foot.'

'Did you really!' cried Sally, admiringly.

'Yes, I dipped it in the inkpot, and I made a mark on the paper. It was a lovely mark, Sally, all black and wet.'

'Some people who can't write, like old Widow Watkins in the cottage, make a mark, too, Sam. They dip their pen in the ink and make a cross. I know, for I heard missis talking about it.'

'My mark got on the carpet, Sally. I hurried away,' said Sam. 'But this letter now. Tell me more.'

'I don't know any more, Sam,' said Sally, patiently. 'You want pen and ink and paper, and then you can write a letter.'

'I shall write to Farmer Greensleeves, to cheer him up. He looks rather sorry sometimes. I think he is sad when it rains so much,' said Sam. 'I love Farmer Greensleeves, but not Mrs Greensleeves. She says, "There's that pig again. Don't let him come in the house. Keep him away from here." I won't write a letter to her. I'll send her a bill. I'll write a nice kind letter to Master, for he's very kind to me.'

There were footsteps in the lane and Sam slid down from the wall. Sally turned, and they watched the gap between the trees.

'Postman's steps,' said Sally. 'He's coming back this way. Ask him, Sam.'

Sally gave a whinny of recognition and trotted across the field to the corner by the lane. The postman stopped to stroke the Mare's nose. He took an apple out of his pocket, and held it out to her.

'Good old Sally,' said he. Then he caught sight of young Sam, peeping over the wall.

'That a friend of yours, Sally?' he asked, and Sally whinnied again.

'Sam Pig,' said Sally, introducing Sam.

'Please, Mr Postman,' said Sam, slowly and clearly, so that the man would understand. 'I want to write a letter for the post. I don't know where to get any real paper. They won't take birch bark, will they?'

'No, Sam Pig,' said the postman. 'You can buy paper at the Post Office in the village, and ink too.'

'The shop where Brock bought his fireworks for bonfire night?' asked Sam.

'Yes. Our Post Office sells most things,' said the postman. 'You'll find all you want there. Mrs Bunting's a kind-hearted woman. You go with your money and ask her nicely.' He shouldered his bag and went on his way.

Sam went home and told Brock the Badger all about it.

'Why all this desire for letter-writing all of a sudden, Sam?' asked Brock, sucking at his pipe and looking down at the bright eyes of little Sam Pig. Ann came close to her brother and pulled at his sleeve. Tom and Bill were not there, or Sam would not have spoken so freely.

'I think you could write a lovely letter, Sam,' said she.

'What is it all about?' asked Brock.

'I would like to write a letter for the postman to take to Farmer Greensleeves to cheer him up. He only gets bills, except at Christmas and birthdays. I would like to write to lots of people.'

Sam spoke very earnestly, and Brock was impressed.

'You will want pen and ink and paper,' said he.

'Yes. The postman said I could buy them at the

village shop, but Brock, I don't want to go there. I'm
afraid of all the people and the boys. I'm going to the
Big House, Brock.'

'All right, Sam. Take care of yourself,' said Brock,
calmly. 'The village shop is really my place, not
yours. I am stout and strong, like a workman, but you
are little and fat. Besides, I remember the village boys
once caught you and made you into a Guy Fawkes.
Yes, better try the Big House first.'

Sam set off for the Big House, with his stick in his
hand, his fiddle and bow under his arm, and a present
of a bag of walnuts for the Irish cook. The lodge gate
was open and he walked through, but the lodge-
keeper called after him.

'Hi, there! Come back, you young varmint! Who
do you think you are, walking up the drive to the
House as if you owned it?' shouted the man, shaking
his fist at Sam.

'It's me, sir! Sam Pig!' said Sam. 'Have you forgotten me already? It's only me.'

'Oh, it's you, is it, Sam Pig?' said the lodge-keeper.
'You who found our silver for us. I thought it was
one of those fiddling lads. Yes, you can pass, Sam Pig.
I didn't remember you at first. How are you keeping,
Sam?'

'Quite well, thank you,' said Sam, politely. 'I am
going to see my friend, the Irish cook.'

Sam trotted swiftly up the long drive, but he
turned away from the big front door of the great

house. Instead, he went along the terrace and looked in the french windows of the library. He could see the writing-table and the blotter, the books on the walls and the leather-seated chairs, but today somebody was sitting at the table. Sam slipped past like a shadow, and went round by the stables to the back door. He crept along the stone passage to the kitchen and there he tapped.

'Tap! Tap! Tap!' went his little knuckles.

'Somebody at the door, Cook. Shall I go?' asked a girl.

'Yes, me darlin'. See who it is. Say I'm busy,' answered the cook, and Sam smiled with pleasure to hear the warm Irish voice.

There was a patter of feet and the door was flung open by one of the kitchen maids.

'Why, it's that little Pigling, as came here before, Cook,' she cried.

'Ask him in! Welcome! Faith! And it's my own wee Pigwiggin come to see me,' said the cook, raising her floury arms from a great bowl and running to look at Sam.

Sam came forward shyly and the maids surrounded him. One took off his hat and scratched his ears, another tweaked his curly tail and the cook popped a lump of sugar in his open mouth.

'Welcome, Pigwiggin,' said she again. 'It's many a long day since we saw you. Shure you've grown stouter! Where have you been all this time?'

'I've been playing about and helping Brock and ... and ... learning my alphabet,' said Sam.

'Indade, now. That's a clever pig you are,' said she.

'And now I want some notepaper and a pen, please,' said Sam. 'There's some in that room with the books, and I want some, please.'

'That's not for you, nor for me, little Pigwiggin,' said the cook, 'but I'll tell you what I'll do. I've a box of notepaper upstairs and I'll give you some.'

She turned to one of the kitchen maids. 'Just fetch my paper and envelopes down, and I'll give some to Sam Pig.'

'Let you sit here, Sam, and have a drink of cocoa and a currant bun with me while she's after fetchin' it. You can tell me all the news.'

So Sam sat on a stool and told all the news of his own little world; about Sally the Mare, and Brock the Badger, and Ann and Tom and Bill.

He put his fiddle under his chin and played an Irish jig and the two little kitchen maids danced on the stone floor while the Cook hummed and clapped her hands.

He helped to stir the pudding, and he took a hand in cleaning the silver. He licked out the pudding bowl, and he drank all the cream left in the cream jug. The cook stuffed his pockets with cakes, and one kitchen maid gave him a ribbon for Sister Ann, and the other gave him a penny whistle.

With the notepaper and envelopes under his arm,

he went away, and it wasn't until he got home and put the paper on the table that he remembered he had no pen and ink.

'A pen is easy enough,' said Brock. 'The grey goose at the farm will give you a feather, and you can cut a pen from it. That's the best kind of pen, a quill. Ink is not so easy.'

'Molly the dairymaid will give me a bottle of ink,' said Sam. 'I am sure she will.'

Molly was busy in the dairy when little Sam went to make his request.

'Ink? Ink?' cried Molly. 'Surely you aren't going to drink it, Sam?'

'Certainly not, Molly. I want it to ... to ...' stammered Sam.

'To write a letter, of course. That's the proper thing to do with ink. I'll fetch my penny bottle in a minute, but mind you don't drop it or lose it or spill it,' said she.

'Can I turn the handle of the churn while you fetch it?' asked Sam.

'Yes, you can, young Sam. Keep it moving or the butter won't come. I won't be more than a minute,' replied Molly, and she hurried out of the dairy, down the passage to the staircase. When she got upstairs to her quiet bedroom she couldn't resist sitting down and writing a letter to her sweetheart. She forgot all about Sam and the butter-making.

Sam turned the handle and turned the handle, and

after a time there was a little thumping noise inside the churn, which showed that the butter was form-ing.

'Come butter, come. Come butter, come,' he sang in his thin, reedy voice, and he went on with the butter-making song.

> *'Come butter, come.*
> *Come butter, come.*
> *Peter, Paul, let it fall.*
> *Come butter, come.'*

He opened the churn and looked inside. The pale gold butter lay there in the butter-milk. He took out a lump and ate it.

'Oh, lovely butter,' murmured Sam.

He took another piece and he laid it on a board. He kneaded it and pressed it and shaped it like a little gold pig.

'Oh, lovely pigling! Oh, butter pigling,' he sang, and he stuck a few flowers from a mug on the table round its neck.

His voice reached Mrs Greensleeves in the kitchen.

'My goodness! There's a pig in the dairy I do be-lieve,' she cried, hurrying along the passage.

'Oh! Oh! Sam Pig! Whatever are you doing here?' she exclaimed, and she took Sam by the ears and lifted him squealing from the table.

Molly came running downstairs with the bottle of ink.

'See who's in the dairy,' cried Mrs Greensleeves, indignantly.

'It's all my fault, Missis,' said Molly. 'I told him to churn for me while I went upstairs for the ink. The butter's come. He always has a good butter-hand, has Sam Pig.'

'Look what he's made,' said Mrs Greensleeves, still rather upset.

'It's quite a good butter-pig,' laughed Molly, and she gave the bottle of ink to Sam, who was hesitating at the door.

'Here, take it, Sam, and don't forget to let me have it back when you've written your letter,' said she.

'Written your letter?' echoed Mrs Greensleeves. 'What next? You'll encourage that pig till there's no bearing with him.'

Sam didn't wait for more. He ran off with the bottle of ink, and he was half-way across the field when he remembered he had no pen. Of course a pointed stick would do quite well, but this was to be a special letter.

He called to the grey goose who was basking there.

'Grey goose! Will you give me a quill for a pen?' he asked.

'A feather for a pen? I am proud to do it, Sam,' said the grey goose, and she showed Sam where a fine quill lay which she had shed that morning.

Sam sharpened his pocket-knife and cut the quill

to a good point. He dipped the point in the bottle of
ink and the goose stood near to watch him.

'I could write a few words on your back,' said Sam
to the goose, but she shook her head.

'Oh no, Sam! Take your pen and ink home,' said
she.

Sam went off home to his bedroom. That was the
best place for letter-writing. Downstairs Bill and
Tom would mock at him, and out-of-doors there

were too many beetles and butterflies to interrupt by sitting on the white paper.

Sam put a piece of paper on the small table by his bed, he dipped the quill in the ink and he prepared to write a letter.

'Dear Master ...' (He wrote in capital letters, crooked and uneven, but of a beautiful blackness that gave Sam great satisfaction.)

> *'I send U a shillin.*
> *I hop U are willin.*
> *To buy U a pressen*
> *From your luvin Sam.'*

He copied it again, making each letter as clear as possible. Then he addressed the envelope, with great care, writing with his little pink tongue sticking out and his head on one side.

'Master Greensleeves,' he wrote, groaning over the long word. He knew how to spell that for it was on all the farm carts and he had often spelled it out with Sally, but it took a long time to make all those letters in the name.

'G for Goblin,' murmured Sam.

'R for Rain. Oh dear, I don't want it to rain.

'E for Eggs. That's better, that's like a farm.

'E for more Eggs.

'N for Nest. Yes, he'll like that, too.

'S for Sally. That's very good.

'L for Lambs. Yes, Master likes letter L.

'E for Eggs again.

'E for Eggs again. Lots of eggs.

'V for Velvety.

'E for Eggs again. What a lot of eggs for him.

'S for Sally again.'

Sam paused breathless and wiped the pen on his ears, and rubbed his inky fingers on his head. Then he dipped the quill in the ink and went on with the address.

Home Farm.
Hardwick.

He looked at it. He fanned it in the sunshine to dry it and then he put the letter in the envelope. He was so excited, he was trembling. Downstairs he dashed, thumping on each stair as if he would break it.

'Brock, Ann, Tom, Bill,' he shouted, waving the letter above his head. 'Look what I've done. I've writ a letter! I've wrote a letter! My first real letter, all by myself, on paper with real ink.'

'Was that you upstairs?' asked Tom, sarcastically. 'I thought there was an elephant chained in the bedroom. I was going to ask Brock to get a gun and shoot it.'

'Let me look,' said Brock, kindly, and he took the letter.

'Why, you've done it very well, Sam. You are quite a scholar. Each letter well formed. I can read it easily.'

Brock read it aloud to the brothers and sister who

were really proud of Sam, for they couldn't write a word.

'Dear Master,
> *I send U a shillin.*
> *I hop U are willin.*
> *To buy U a pressen*
> *From your luvin Sam.'*

'Very good! But where's the shilling?' asked Bill.

'Will you give me one, Brock? One of those Queen Elizabeth shillings you found in that crock of gold,' asked Sam.

Brock opened the holly-wood money-box and took out a silver shilling with a cross on one side and the Queen on the other. Sam slipped it in the envelope and licked the seal.

'There! There! All ready for the postman,' said he.

'Stop a moment, Sam,' said Brock. 'We must put a special seal on it, because it has money inside. Wait a moment.'

The Badger climbed on the stool and looked on his own private shelf. He took down a piece of sealing-wax, made of the gum of the spruce tree. It was scented like the woods and golden-brown. Brock pressed a small portion on the letter and then he took one of the shillings and stamped the sealing wax with it, so that a little picture of the Queen appeared embedded in the wax.

'That's to keep it quite safe,' said he.

'How lovely!' sighed Ann. 'A real letter, signed and sealed.'

'But not stamped,' said Brock the Badger, suddenly. 'All letters have to be stamped with the head of our King, and I haven't a stamp!'

They all looked at one another.

'I could draw one,' said Sam, hopefully.

'I don't think the postman would like that,' remarked Brock, sadly. 'I shall have to go to Mrs Bunting's and buy one.'

Brock went to the village at dusk and bought a stamp at the village shop. Dogs sniffed at his heels, people stared at the stout little man with a pipe in his mouth, but nobody spoke to him. While he was gone Sam ran across the fields with the bottle of ink and put it on the dairy windowsill. There Molly would find it, he knew. He didn't want to venture indoors again.

Then he went to the stable to tell Sally all about it.

'I written a letter to Master,' said he. 'I written it. I wroted it. I did it. I'm sending him a present, so that he won't mind if it rains.'

'Good little Sam,' smiled Sally. 'I am sure he will be glad.'

So the letter was properly stamped and Sam took it to the pillar-box at the bottom of the lane. He stood on a stone to reach, and he dropped the letter down, down into the deep hole. He stood there some time, waiting and watching for the postman to come.

At last there were footsteps and the whistling postman came down the road. He stopped at the pillarbox and found his keys and opened the door. Sam was so excited he crept near to watch.

There was only one letter, and that was Sam's. The postman took it out, and examined it. Sam crept nearer, and at last he could contain himself no longer.

'Mr Postman, I wrote that letter,' said he.

'Did you indeed, Sam Pig!' cried the postman. 'I can see it is no ordinary letter. It's so well written, I could read it in the dark.'

'Could you?' Sam was delighted.

'There's something inside it, Sam,' said the post-man, pinching the envelope.

'Yes, a present,' said Sam, breathlessly.

'Well, I'll take care of it. I shall deliver it myself later on. Goodbye, Sam.'

The postman went away with the precious letter in his bag, and Sam, after another look at the pillar-box, went home.

The next day he went to talk to Sally in the field.

'Did Master get my letter, Sally?' he asked.

'He did! He *was* pleased! He was right-down pleased. He said he was going to hang the silver shilling on his watch-chain, for luck. He said it was a good letter, well written and all. You've done it this time, Sam.'

Sally was so enthusiastic, Sam felt rather shy. But the Farmer came out and saw them talking together.

'Sam,' said he, holding out his big brown hand and taking Sam's little horny paw in it. 'Sam. You've done me a power of good. I've been worried about the weather and bills and poor crops, but now if things go wrong, I shall look at the silver shilling on my watch-chain, and just laugh. I shall laugh, and be merry, like you, Sam. For I am sure your Queen Elizabeth shilling will bring me luck.'

Sam Pig and the Boggart

One evening as dusk began to fill the woods, and the birds were going home to their nests, Sam Pig remembered that he too had to go home. He had been visiting Sally the Mare, and the time had passed so pleasantly with one story after another, with laughter and jokes, that Sam quite forgot there was a good stretch of field and wood between Sally's warm stable and his own fireside where Ann Pig, Tom Pig, Bill Pig and Brock the Badger were waiting for him. When the sun went down and the air became colder, Sam gave a shiver and looked over the stable door.

'You'd best be off home, little Sam,' said Sally, shaking her mane from her eyes and gazing at the woods. 'You'll be in the dark, and you haven't a lantern. Would you like the stable lantern?'

'No, thank you, Sally. I'm not afraid. I've often been out by myself at night. At least I've been out a few times. Once I met the Fox and once I met the King of the Icicles, and once I went to Babylon by candlelight.' Sam opened the door and stood in the yard, and again he stared at the dark woods.

'Only a bit of moon tonight,' said Sally, nodding

to the thin new moon, and Sam and Sally both bowed in honour of the Queen of the Sky.

'Goodnight, Sally,' said Sam. 'See you tomorrow.'

'Goodnight, Sam,' replied Sally, frisking her tail and shaking her head in a kindly salute. 'Brock will be waiting for you. Go home quickly. Here's a piece of turnip to eat on the way.'

'Thank you, Sally. I expect Tom will have eaten all the supper. Thank you,' said Sam, but still he hesitated, and both animals breathed the sweet night air and listened to the sounds of evening. The barn owl was calling, 'Tu-whit, tu-whoo,' the swifts were crying high in the sky, the bit-bat was squeaking and a nightjar was whirring in the deep grasses where she had her nest.

'Sally,' said Sam. 'Brock stays up all night. Why can't I?'

'A badger is a night animal and you're a day animal like me. He is dark coloured, and his head is striped with black and white like shadows. But you, my little Sam, are very pink. All pink animals go home. Now be off at once.'

So away went Sam, but he stopped a minute in the ploughfield to daub himself with a fistful of soil. He made stripes on his face and dark marks on his legs.

'Now I'm a badger,' said he. Strangely enough he felt bolder with these smudges, and he skipped along and even whistled a song to give himself courage.

But the darkness came down very quickly, and shadows sidled with stealthy movements from behind the trees. Hosts of shadows came from the woods and every bush changed to a hostile and strange creature.

Then Sam thought of a tale Joe Scarecrow had once told him. It was the tale of a boggart that flapped its black wings and wailed, 'Whoo-oo-oo' in the deep, dark night. The scarecrow and Sam had been sitting cosily in a hole in the road, with a red lantern for company, and as the scarecrow talked Sam had felt queer in his stomach. His teeth chattered and a shiver came to his fat little body as he heard of the black boggart. But he hadn't really been afraid with the scarecrow for company. Now it was different, he was all alone with a wide wood between him and his home.

> *'Dragons and goblins,*
> *Boggarts and ghosts,*
> *Unicorns, pussy-cats,*
> *Witches on posts,'*

murmured Sam.

He looked back over his shoulder, and this was very unwise. Never look back if you are afraid, but walk bravely on. Sam looked back, and he thought he saw a black shadow following him. He looked again, and he saw something there. It had long arms, a humped back and flapping black wings. It ran with wavering steps, sideways and even backwards, leaping, darting and stooping to pick up sticks and stones.

'Oh dear. A boggart,' thought Sam. 'Now what can I do? I've never seen one before. Oh dear.'

His legs began to wobble, and his heart beat so fast he could hear it thumping against his ribs. He stopped against a bush, unable to run any more.

The boggart came gliding along the pathway. It put out a thin arm, grabbed Sam and popped him in a sack.

Then on it went, slithering and gliding, with no nice noisy steps, no ordinary animal trot. Sam shivered in the blackness of the bag. He thought of Sally the Mare, and Brock the Badger, and little Ann waiting for him, and he thought of Farmer Greensleeves. He hadn't been so frightened since he was stolen by Man and carried off long ago when he was a tiny pigling. He tried to call out but he had lost even his squeak. His tail was uncurled and his hair was damp.

Suddenly Sam heard the thud of feet on the grass and the swish of branches as somebody pushed through the undergrowth. There was a growl and a snort, and Sam knew it was Brock the Badger.

'Brock. Brock. Save me,' he called, but his voice had gone and only a whimper came from the bag.

'Boggart. What have you got in that sack?' called the deep voice of Brock.

'Only a bag of bones,' whined the boggart, shaking the sack so hard that Sam rattled against the sticks and stones and made a clatter like a lot of bones.

'Take care, boggart. Don't you be frightening anybody,' said Brock.

'Nobody's frightened of me. I'm only a boggart,' said the boggart, and it loped away into the shadows, leaving the good-hearted Brock staring after it.

'I thought I heard something,' murmured Brock. 'I thought I heard a whimper. But Sam's safely at home. No, it can't be Sam.'

He went on through the woods, for Brock loved the early moon and the smell of the woodlands and the darkness.

Sam wept a little tear when Brock was left behind. He wept so hard that his voice came back and he called out to the boggart.

'Boggart. What are you going to do with me?' he asked.

'Eat you,' said the boggart, in a husky, dusky voice.

'If you eat me, then Brock the Badger will come after you with a big stick,' warned Sam, boldly.

The boggart stopped and threw down the sack, and Sam crept out.

'Brock the Badger will never know,' said the boggart, sitting on a tree stump and licking its black lips.

Quite near them Sam could see a gate he knew, and the gate led to a field and in the field lived a friend.

'Please, boggart, will you take me to that ploughed field?' asked Sam. 'There are turnips growing in that field and pork and turnips go well together.'

'Quite true,' whispered the boggart, and it bundled

Sam back in the sack and ran swiftly to the ploughed field.

'I'll get some turnips,' said the boggart.

'Please, boggart, you can put me down by that ragged man of straw, that scarecrow thing,' said Sam. 'You can tie me to his wooden leg so that I can't escape. I'm bruised in this sack, with the sticks and stones.'

'All right,' said the boggart, and it carried Sam to Joe Scarecrow, who stood dreaming in the middle of the field.

'Now here's a go, and no mistake,' sighed the scarecrow. 'A boggart. Oh, dear me, a boggart.'

The boggart tossed the sack at the scarecrow's foot and Sam rolled out. The scarecrow stood there unblinking, saying nothing at all, and it took no notice of Sam.

'I'll fasten you to this wooden leg,' said the boggart to Sam. 'Stay here till I'm ready.'

It tied Sam up and then with the sack on its back it ran about the fields gathering turnips. Farmer Greensleeves, who was out with his gun, saw the shadow wandering there, and he turned away uneasily.

'Boggart's about tonight,' said he to himself. 'Only a silver bullet can catch a boggart, they say.'

Little Tim Rabbit saw the boggart there and he ran home very fast to tell his mother.

The Fox saw the boggart wavering about in the

field and he hurried into the covert, for boggarts and men were his enemies.

'Sam,' whispered Joe Scarecrow. 'What's amiss? What are you doing here, away from home in the dark night? Just look at that boggart, running about. What are you doing, Sam?'

The scarecrow raised its long wooden leg and let the rope slip. Sam lay at Joe Scarecrow's foot, not daring to move.

'Help me, Joe,' he murmured. 'I'm awful scared. Can't run away even if I try.'

'Has the boggart got you, Sam?' asked the scarecrow, and Sam nodded.

'I'll help you, Sam,' said the scarecrow. 'There's only one way to deal with a boggart and that's to scare him, too.'

He stooped with his long wooden arm and picked up a turnip from the soil. In a moment he had scooped out the centre. He took a candle from the folds of his ragged coat, and a match from the box in his torn trouser pocket.

Sam stared with wide eyes at Joe Scarecrow's movements.

'What a good thing the shepherd keeps his matches here,' remarked the scarecrow, who suddenly seemed unafraid. 'He hides a box of matches and candle in my ragged clothes so that he can always find them when he's out in the fields. I keep them dry for him. Match box is wrapped in a piece of sheepskin, and there's a pipe, too, and a bit of baccy.'

While he spoke he put the candle in the hollow turnip, and lit it. Then he held it under his coat and waited for the boggart. Sam shivered with excitement. His courage had returned, he was happy to be with the scarecrow.

'When that wandering creature comes back here Sam, you let out an awful screech like the owl hunting, or a rabbit with a stoat after it, and I'll hold up this turnip face. If I can scare crows, I can surely scare a boggart. Now keep brave, Sam. It likes you to be afraid, but if you are brave you'll get free from the creature.'

They watched the boggart stooping here and there, choosing nice juicy turnips and popping them in the sack. Then it came with a wavering slanting step back to the scarecrow, and Sam's silvery hairs stood upright with panic, and his nose was cold as ice.

'Worse than the King of the Icicles,' he thought. The scarecrow was behind him, waiting, and Sam took courage again from that heart of wood and straw, that bold figure who stayed all night in the fields braving every terror to keep the Farmer's corn from harm.

'Come along, Sam Pig,' said the boggart. 'Come with me. Roast pig and boiled turnips is my fancy tonight. I've never had such a feast, but I've never caught a fat young pig before. Thank you for reminding me of the turnips.'

It waved its flapping black arms, and dived towards Sam, but at that moment the scarecrow brought out the goblin face of the turnip lantern and waved it in the boggart's path. Sam gave a blood-curdling screech – he had no need to imitate either the screech-owl or the rabbit, it was the natural cry of a terrified little pig. The boggart started back. It went further back, shaking its flapping arms, hiding its face in the folds of shadowy cloth. Then with a shrill wail it fled, across the field and into the woods, far away to the haunted house where it lived. As it ran it mumbled to itself, 'Worser than me. Something blinked and winked at me, out of a turnip face.'

'Saved, little Sam,' said the scarecrow to Sam, who was clinging to the wooden leg. 'The boggart has turned tail. You are safe now. It won't come back. It has gone down in the earth.'

'Please, Joe Scarecrow, can I stay with you all night?' pleaded Sam.

'Of course you can, little Sam. You curl up at my foot and I'll wrap my coat around you,' said the scarecrow, kindly. 'See, I'll put the lighted turnip near you, and nothing will come.'

Even as they spoke, there was a thump, thump of feet and Brock the Badger came trotting swiftly over the ploughfield.

'Here you are, Sam. I've been hunting for you. I thought the boggart had caught you, for when I got home, Ann said you were lost. Then Sally the Mare told me you had started hours ago. What are you doing here?'

'The boggart did catch me, Brock,' said Sam. 'I tried to call out, and you never heard.'

'Poor Sam! Was it you after all? I thought there was something in the boggart's sack. Now let me give you a word of advice. Never run away from a boggart. Always stand firm and face it, and scare it away. You get ready first, Sam, and then it can't touch you.'

Brock turned to the silent scarecrow, who stood

waiting there, rather disappointed that Brock had come.

'Joe Scarecrow, I want to thank you for looking after little Sam. I shall bring you a present, Joe. Sam and I won't forget your kindness.'

The scarecrow mumbled shyly, and Sam and Brock said goodnight. They padded quietly away across the field, through the woods and fields to their home. Everyone was in bed but a candle was burning on the window-sill. Sam drank a bowl of milk and then he rolled into his own small bed and fell asleep.

'Poor old Sam,' murmured Brock, covering him up. 'He has had a fright, but it won't harm him. It will help him to be brave.'

The next day they went off to the ploughfield. The scarecrow was flapping his hands and the rooks were cawing and flying away from him.

Brock carried a little wooden clacker for the scarecrow and a warm scarf to wrap round his neck.

'Thank you, Mr Brock,' said the scarecrow, wrapping himself in the rough red wool. 'I get a touch of rheumatics later on at the back end of the year. It's chilly at nights. Would you like a puff of the shepherd's baccy, Mr Brock?'

Brock said he would be delighted to taste Man's baccy, and Joe Scarecrow drew the old pipe from his pocket and gave Brock a light from the box of matches.

So Brock sat there, smoking for half an hour, and

Joe Scarecrow swung the clacker to scare away the birds. Sam sang the bird-scaring song, and every rook and crow, magpie and jay perched on the wall to listen.

'Ho! little birds,
Now fly away do,
Or Joe the Scarecrow
Will moggrify you.'

Then away flew all the birds, right over the fields to the woods.

That night, when it was dark as pitch, for the little new moon was hidden, and no light came from the stars, that night Brock came out of the house of the Four Pigs and walked with his determined trot across the fields to the haunted house.

'Boggart. Come out,' he called, but there was no answer. 'Boggart, come out,' he called again, and there was a faint rustle in the doorway.

'Boggart, come out,' shouted Brock, and this time the darkness was filled with shadowy movements and the boggart came before Brock, bowing and curtseying, in an apologetic manner.

'Boggart,' said Brock, sternly. 'You must not frighten any young creatures. Keep your visits for robbers and thieves. Frighten the bad ones, and leave the young innocents in peace. Keep a watch for robbers and evil-doers, and wave your long arms at them to frighten them away. Then, boggart, you will be helping the world to go round.'

'Yes, Brock the Badger,' murmured the boggart. 'I will do as you say, if only you will let me live here in the haunted house.'

'Certainly,' said Brock. 'You must have a home, old boggart. Here you shall live, and take your ease, but remember what I've told you.'

'Yes, Brock the Badger,' said the boggart, humbly.

'And if you go on with good deeds,' continued Brock, hopefully, 'you may change from a boggart to a good spirit, one never knows.'

'Yes, Brock the Badger,' said the boggart, who was not quite sure whether he wanted to be as good as all that.

'Well, goodnight,' said Brock.

'Goodnight, Brock the Badger,' said the boggart, and it went back to the haunted house and sat in the dark kitchen to make a cup of invisible tea and to eat an invisible slice of bread.

Sam Pig Goes to the Fête

Sam Pig was walking home across the fields one afternoon, and he took a short cut past the cottages of a hamlet called Little Green. It was a very small place, with very small cottages, and Sam thought a very small pig would not be noticed. Besides, there was a pig-sty at the end of one of the gardens, and he wanted to say a word of encouragement and cheer to the fat little pig within.

He crept up to the sty, but the little pig was snoring indoors and it wouldn't come out to play.

Near a cottage gate a white goat was chained, and Sam stopped a minute to look at her. Sam was not very friendly with goats, since long ago a Billy-goat had come to live in Brock the Badger's house when Brock was away from home, but this was a Nanny with a silky coat.

'Good evening,' said the little white goat, shaking her head and ringing her bell. 'Good evening, Sam Pig.'

'Good evening, Nanny,' said Sam, pleased to hear her shrill little Baa-aa-aa.

'Are you coming tomorrow?' asked the goat.

'Where?' asked Sam. 'I'm coming here and there as usual.'

'There's going to be a Fête,' said the goat, and she took a nibble at the hedge and danced on her hind legs in a way Sam admired.

Sam stared at her. He didn't understand, but he was not going to ask the little white goat what she meant.

'Are you going, Nanny?' he asked.

'No. I'm fastened to this stake, but you can go. You are free,' replied the Nanny-goat.

'Not as free as you think,' said Sam, cautiously. 'I've got my family to consider. Brock the Badger, and Ann, Bill and Tom are my family. I can't go everywhere.'

'There'll be a sack race,' said the Nanny, contentedly chewing. 'I've seen children practising with them, Sam Pig. Surely you would like that.'

'Oh,' said Sam. 'A sack race. I never knew sacks could run. Farmer Greensleeves makes sacks stay where he puts 'em.'

'These sacks race,' said the Nanny. 'I saw some of Farmer Greensleeves' sacks lying ready.'

Sam was very much puzzled, but still he didn't ask questions.

'There's a three-legged race,' said the Nanny, and she took a sudden bite of the grass, and the long streamers dipped from her mouth like green whiskers so that Sam Pig nearly burst out laughing as he looked at her.

'I can do a three-legged race,' said Sam. 'But I wonder where children find that extra leg. They have only two, poor things.'

'There's an obstacle race,' said the Nanny.

'What's an obstacle?' asked Sam, who was completely bewildered by all this information.

'Something that gets in the way,' said the Nanny.

'Like the fox?' asked Sam, hopefully.

'Like anything that bothers you, same as this chain,' said the Nanny, shaking her tethering chain.

'When is this Fête?' asked Sam.

'Tomorrow. Baa-baa-baa,' bleated the goat, and she turned her head in warning. A little girl was coming from the cottage. Sam took to his heels and disappeared in the hedge, from which he watched her.

The little girl carried some sheets of paper with words written on them in black letters, all crooked as if Sam himself had written them. She tacked one of the notices to a tree, and stood back to admire it. Then on she went to another tree, and fastened a paper on the rough bark.

Sam couldn't resist coming out and peeping at the white paper, so smooth and clean. With a great effort he spelt it.

'TO THE FETE,' he read. An arrow pointed to a field. He followed the child and watched her tack notices to all the trees, to a gate and a stile. They all said the same thing; they all pointed to the field.

Then Sam turned away and galloped home, bursting with excitement.

'Ann, Bill, Tom, Brock the Badger,' he shouted, as he dashed into the little house. 'Brock! There's a Fête at Little Green tomorrow. Brock, I want to go. Is there any money in the money-box?'

'Good gracious, Sam. What are you talking about?' said Tom, crossly. 'Why do you want money? Why did you run off this afternoon instead of gardening and helping us?'

'What's a Fête?' asked little Ann Pig, dropping her mending and looking at her brother.

'It's sack racing and obstacles and three-legged racing. I can run on three legs,' said Sam, very quickly.

'Who told you?' asked Brock, quietly, and the Badger put down his green notebook and smiled at Sam.

'The Nanny-goat, Brock, but I read it, in words, on some trees. A little girl was putting notices on trees, just like I do, but I write on the tree and she writes on paper, white as snow with big black letters, like mine,' said Sam, hurriedly.

'Then it must be true,' said Bill. 'All printing is true when it's on paper. Not when it's on sand or earth like yours, Sam.'

'Can we all go?' asked Ann.

'I don't want to go,' grumbled Tom Pig. 'Too risky, with all those children about.'

'Nor me,' said Bill. 'You may get put in a pie and eaten, Sam.'

'I want to go with Sam,' said little Ann Pig quickly. 'I will take care of him and he will take care of me. We can both run very fast. Do you remember when we went to the Flower Show?'

Brock slowly took two silver shillings from the holly-wood money-box on the mantelpiece. He looked at them carefully and turned them round. They were Queen Elizabeth shillings, with the fine face of the Tudor Queen. Brock had dug them up one day in the pasture, where there was a hoard hidden for nearly four hundred years in a crock of gold. The crock he kept for drinking his barley ale, and the silver shillings filled the money-box.

'Here's the money, Sam. You two can go, I can trust you, but do be careful. I don't want to come and rescue you.'

'Oh, yes, we'll be careful,' promised Sam and Ann together, and they clasped hands and danced round the table, to the frowns of Tom and Bill.

The next day Sam and Ann got ready very early. Sam wore his wide-brimmed hat, and Ann wore a sun-bonnet to conceal her ears. Sam's check trousers had been washed and ironed, and Ann had put on her Sunday frock, with a frill round the hem and a frill round her little pink neck.

They tucked roses in their buttonholes, and set off,

with the shillings firmly held in their fists, and clean handkerchiefs in their pockets.

They went to the hamlet of Little Green, keeping to the hedgerows, and walking very softly. There they read the notices tacked to the trees. Somebody had put an extra word underneath.

'2.30 p.m.,' it said.

'We're too soon, Ann,' said Sam. 'Let's go there and look about before the people come.'

They walked through the open gate into the field, and sat in the shade of a gorse-bush to watch the preparations. They saw the wooden pegs knocked in the ground and the rope put round to mark the racecourse. There were wooden stalls and tables on trestles and baskets of cups and saucers placed ready on the grass. A heap of sacks lay under a tree, and a bran tub stood by a cherry tree, with some skipping ropes and mallets and a dart-board, a sack of flour and a bucket of water.

'We didn't bring any dinner,' said Sam, suddenly, feeling very empty. 'I'm hungry.'

'So am I, Sam,' said Ann. 'We shall have to eat grass, there's nothing else here. I thought there would be plenty of food.'

The villagers went home to have their dinners and the field was empty, except for the two little pigs who sat sedately under their gorse-bush, unseen and unheard. Then out they came, stepping softly, with glances around.

'Let's taste the bran tub,' said Sam, and he dipped a hand inside and took up a heap of the brown flakes. It was delicious and Ann joined him.

'I likes bran,' said Ann, smacking her lips.

Next they found the apples and ate a few, and they drank from the bucket of water.

'I feel better now,' said Sam, as they strolled on and examined the dart-board. They were just going to play when they saw somebody coming, so they sat on the heap of sacks with Farmer Greensleeves' name upon them, and waited for the Fête to begin.

People trickled back to the field, carrying baskets of cakes and buns for the tea stall, garments for the jumble sale, toys for the bran tub, and apples and groceries for the other stalls. They were so busy arranging their goods that they did not notice two little creatures shuffling among the sacks. The little pigs wrapped sacks around themselves and stood up.

'They hide our feet,' whispered Ann, laughing.

'Nobody would know we are different,' smiled Sam, looking at himself. 'Let's join the others.'

Several children were walking about, tasting the ice cream, looking at the stalls, and Sam and Ann trotted lightly through the Fête.

'It's not the sack-race yet,' somebody remarked.

Sam Pig bent his head and kept his nose hidden, but his blue eyes were spying around, and little shivers of delight ran down his spine.

'Oh, Ann,' he whispered. 'It's as good as the Flower Show.'

'Yes, Sam,' Ann murmured. 'Yes. Let's go and see what is over there, where the crowd is.'

They tripped gaily across the grass to the jumble sale and stood quietly watching the people who shook old garments and held them up for inspection.

Sam saw a pair of old trousers which would just do for Brock. He put his hand in his pocket and brought out his shilling. He pointed to the trousers.

'How much, please?' he asked, keeping his voice as low as possible.

'Let me see,' said the busy woman. 'Those old things. You can have them for threepence, little boy. Are they for your dad? He won't say thank you for them. Better give them to a scarecrow.'

'I will,' said Sam, thinking of poor Joe, out in the fields.

The helper changed Sam's ancient coin, without a glance at it, and she gave Sam nine pennies back. Then she turned to others who were calling and holding up hats and shoes and coats.

'Look, Ann,' said Sam, softly. 'Look what I've got. She gave me all these pennies, too. You have a try, Ann.'

So Sam stood away in the background and little Ann went timidly to the stall, squeezing among the village women. She picked up a hat with faded roses on it, and waved it with her silver coin. She wasn't very good at talking to people.

'You can have that for threepence, my dear,' said a kind woman, and she took Ann's money and dropped it in the basin without noticing its age and beauty. Little Ann danced away with the flowery hat and a fistful of pence.

'Ann. What have you got? A dish of flowers? A straw plate?' asked Sam, who had never seen such finery.

'It's a Sunday hat,' said Ann, firmly putting it on her head and tossing her sun-bonnet away. 'She gave me lots of pennies, too. I do like a Fête.'

'Come along, Ann. Let's go to the bran. They are all dipping in it and eating it.'

When they arrived they saw that the children were spending pennies, and dipping their hands in the tub. Each child brought up something from the depths.

'Twopence a dip,' said a woman.

'A treasure hunt,' whispered Sam.

He gave up two of his precious pennies, and plunged his arm into the bran. He brought out a parcel tied with string. Carefully he unfolded it, and put the string in his pocket. It would be very useful for fastening things. The paper, too, was precious, and he folded it away.

He had found an ash tray, and he turned it over and examined it with joy.

'What is it?' asked Ann.

'It's a little dish for roast acorns, or for mushrooms, or a few blackberries,' said Sam. 'I shall give it to Tom for his cooking.'

Then Ann dipped into the bran tub and she brought out a packet tied like Sam's with pink string. Inside lay a powder puff.

'What can it be?' she asked, stroking its feathery softness. 'Is it a big dandelion clock? Or a bunch of Traveller's Joy? Is it a flower? Can you eat it?'

'That queer little girl has got a powder puff,' somebody remarked, laughing at the two little pigs whose heads, concealed in their big hats, were bent over the parcel. They stood under a wild plum tree, and the shadows fell down and the golden light of the sun mottled their stout little bodies with flecks of gold and black.

'It's a tickler,' announced Sam, rubbing the puff on Ann's nose till she laughed aloud.

Then Sam had to have another dip, and this time he got a tablet of soap. It had such a sweet scent he took a bite. Oh! Oh! He spat it out and rubbed his mouth.

'It's a piece of soap, Ann. Who would have thought it? I'll take it home for the bath-tub.'

They passed the fruit and vegetable stall, and a woman gave them a couple of apples to eat.

They went on to the ice-cream stall, and there they stopped, watching the children give up their money.

'What are they eating?' asked Ann. 'It looks like snow, but there is no snow in summer.'

'It may be soap froth,' said Sam, hesitating.

The Vicar saw the two little outcasts standing at the edge of the mob of small children.

'Come along, children,' said he. 'Would you like an ice?'

Without waiting for a reply he bought two cones and put them in the outstretched hands of Sam and Ann.

'Thank you, sir,' said Sam, in such a shrill sudden voice that the Vicar jumped with surprise.

'Goodness me! Who are you? Gypsy children? Do you live in a caravan?'

'No, sir. Not now,' said Sam, more quietly.

The Vicar watched for a moment as Sam and Ann licked their ices with the tips of their little pink tongues.

'Oh,' cried Ann, shivering. 'It *is* snow. Sweet snow. Sugary snow. Honey snow.'

'I wish it would always snow like this. All the woods and fields covered with sweet snow. Think of it, Ann. What would Brock say? Bill would go out and fill buckets with it.' Sam was in raptures, but he noticed the Vicar's intent gaze.

'Please, sir, does it always snow like this at a Fête?' he asked.

'What? What?' cried the astonished man. 'I beg your pardon?'

'Does it always snow here?' asked Sam.

'Bless my soul! What is the child talking about? What's your name and where do you come from, boy? Is this your sister?'

'Sam Pig. Ann Pig,' said Sam, rapidly, and he backed away, cautiously.

'Poor creature,' said the Vicar to a lady. 'Very ugly. I could have sworn he was . . . yes, I thought he was . . . But I mustn't judge. I must be charitable. I thought he was . . .' (he lowered his voice to a whisper) '. . . a little pig!'

Sam and Ann were leaping about at the far end of

the field, where they had retreated. They licked their ice creams and sat down on the stones under the old cherry trees.

Boys and girls were getting in line for a race, and they decided to join in, for the Vicar was far away, talking to some of his congregation.

'Whatever you do, you mustn't go on all fours,' said Sam, sternly. 'Run properly and don't go down on your hands, Sister Ann.'

Ann promised she wouldn't, and Sam hid the treasures he had bought in the bushes for safety. Together they went to the race. Unluckily the Vicar came too.

'Race for children under eight,' he called in his fine clerical voice. 'Get into line now. Get ready. When I blow the whistle, then go!'

But when the whistle sounded Ann and Sam never moved from their places. It wasn't until the others had nearly reached the tape that Sam realized what had happened. Off the pair scampered, but they were too late.

'You ought to have got away when the whistle blew,' said an old man. 'You was looking about you.'

Sam hung his head in shame.

Next came the egg-and-spoon race. Sam held his egg in the spoon and Ann held hers. When the Vicar blew his whistle, Sam tossed his egg in the air and swallowed it, shell and all; Ann did the same.

'I won,' said Sam, but again everyone had rushed off to the tape.

'You didn't ought to *eat* your egg,' scolded the old man, who was watching them.

Next was the three-legged race, and Sam saw the others form pairs and tie two legs together.

'So that's what they do,' he sighed, and he took his clean hanky and tied his leg to Ann's.

The Vicar examined the knots, and when he saw Sam's cloven foot and Ann's neat ankle, he gave a faint cry.

'Surely you are . . . you are . . . little pigs?' said he.

'Yes, sir,' said Sam. 'Don't tell on us.'

'Well, no. It's very irregular. I'm at a loss. I'm bewildered,' said the Vicar, and in confusion he blew the whistle.

Immediately everyone began to run, but Sam Pig and Ann Pig flew like the wind and got there first.

'The first prize is won by . . . what are your names?' asked the Vicar again.

'Sam Pig and Ann Pig. We told you, sir,' said Sam.

'Of course,' he murmured, writing down the names. 'I really don't know what to do,' said he to himself.

Then came the sack race. Everyone climbed into a sack, all ready to start. Sam and little Ann, who had tossed their sacks aside, now draped them round their legs. Their strong little hooves moved easily in the sacking, and they felt warm and comfortable.

'I likes wearing a sack,' said Ann in a whisper to her brother.

'There's a nice smell of taters in mine,' said Sam, sniffing.

'Mine had cow-cake,' said Ann.

The whistle blew, and away they went, to the admiration of the old man. Their little trotters scuttled over the grass.

'Well run. Well run,' he cried, clapping his horny palms, as Ann and Sam ran through the tape together.

'Ann Pig. Sam Pig,' said the Vicar, writing down the names. 'You got here exactly together. A curious coincidence. You must divide the prize.'

Ann and Sam said nothing. They hoped they would be allowed to take the sacks home, but the children threw their sacks in a heap, and slowly the two little pigs removed their covering.

'Now it's the obstacle race,' cried all the children, dancing with excitement, and Sam and Ann said, 'Ob . . . stickle. Ob . . . stickle.'

'I hope it won't bite,' said Ann. 'Please hold my hand, Sam.'

'I'll take care of you,' said Sam, clutching his little sister's damp fist.

They watched the grown-ups place the obstacles around the roped space, and they wondered what it could mean. There was a row of empty barrels with no bottoms. Next some buckets of water stood on the grass with apples floating on the surface. Near was a sack of flour.

'Do you think we have to eat all that flour?' asked Ann. 'I don't care for flour. Do you think we have to roll in it?'

Sam shook his head. He was watching the men arrange a fence for all to climb over, and a tablecloth under which all must creep, and a pile of buns which surely were to be eaten.

The children formed up in line and Sam and Ann stood with them, still holding hands. Ann's big hat was awry, and Sam's hat flapped over his face. His check trousers were stained with green, and Ann's clean frock was crumpled and torn.

The whistle blew, and everyone started except the two little pigs, who were bewildered. They ran backwards.

'Quick. Run the other way. Hurry,' the old man cried, giving them a push. 'The obstacle race has begun. You're going the wrong way.'

'I was going for the buns,' explained Sam.

They hurried after the rest, and caught them at the first obstacle. They stood aside and watched, as the children crept through the barrels. That was easy enough, and Sam and Ann sprang through in a flash.

'I like going through barrels,' said Sam.

'So do I,' said Ann. 'I like rolling downhill in a barrel.'

They dipped their faces in the flour and tasted it,

and then they dipped their heads in the bucket and each caught an apple and munched it.

'I like eating apples,' said Sam.

'So do I. I could eat apples all day,' agreed Ann.

They were soon at the head of the race, and they hurried to the fence and climbed over. They came to the sheet, and they crawled under it. It was all too easy.

Finally they reached the heap of buns. They crammed their mouths, and ate with slow contented munches.

'Very nice buns,' said Sam.

'Very nice,' said Ann.

'I 'specks these are the prizes,' said Sam.

'I like prizes with sugar on them,' said Ann.

The buns were fast disappearing when the others came up.

'Stop! Stop! Don't eat all the buns. Only one each! Run to the tape,' shouted a man hurrying to them.

But Sam and Ann were frightened. They raced away through the tape to the corner of the field.

'I think we will go home,' said Ann. 'We've had a good tea.'

'Yes. We'll go home now,' said Sam.

They dived under the bushes and brought out the pair of trousers, the powder puff and the ash tray, with various apples and sweets and balloons which they had bought with their pennies. They shuffled away, through the hedge, past the Nanny-goat, who

was waiting to see them, past the lively little pig in the sty, who was awake and squeaking, past all the cottages of Little Green.

The Vicar was giving the prizes. Names were called, and children came up to the table.

The Vicar called, 'Sam Pig! Ann Pig! First prize for the three-legged race,' but nobody came to claim the prize.

He called, 'Sam Pig! Ann Pig! First prize for the sack race,' but nobody came to claim the prize.

Then he called, 'Sam Pig! Ann Pig! First prize for

the obstacle race,' but nobody came to claim the prize.

'Has anyone seen two little pigs?' he asked, but they all laughed, for they thought he was making a joke.

Sam and Ann were already far away, scampering home to the family.

'Look what I got for Joe Scarecrow,' cried Sam, waving the ancient trousers.

'And I have a little soft brush to tickle your nose, dear Brock,' said Ann. She twiddled the powder puff in the Badger's face, and brushed his nose with flour.

'And a cookery book for Bill,' said Sam. 'I found it in the bran tub. And a piece of soap for Tom to wash with.'

'And a little dish for roast acorns or blackberries,' added Ann, showing them the ash tray.

'What is that thing on your head, Ann?' asked Brock, slowly taking the pipe from his mouth and staring at Ann's flowery hat. The big roses flopped on one side, and a wide ribbon tied it under Ann's chin.

'It's a beautiful hat I bought at the Fête,' said Ann, and she demurely curtsied to her guardian, Brock the Badger.

'The first drop of rain will spoil those roses,' said Brock, sniffing at them. 'No scent. Not like real roses, Ann.'

'We won some prizes,' said Sam, 'but we didn't

stop to carry them away. People were staring because we ate all the buns in the obstacle race.'

'I never knew buns were obstacles,' murmured Brock. 'But you were quite right. Always hurry home when people look too hard at you.'

'Did you enjoy yourselves?' asked Tom, kindly.

'It was beautiful,' sighed Ann. 'We ate sweet snow, which falls there in summer, and we drank ginger beer, and we ate bran in a tub, and apples that floated in a bucket of water, and lots of buns.'

'You won't want any supper,' remarked Bill.

'No, thank you,' said Sam, politely.

'Brock, there was a very strange happening,' said Ann. 'There was a tub of bran. We were going to eat it, but they took our pennies and told us to dip into it. All kinds of things were hidden there. It was a magical tub, with lollypops and marbles and books and games all in the bran, Brock.'

'A magical tub,' said Brock, slowly.

Brock and the Bran Tub

That night little Sam Pig lay awake. He could hear his brothers and sister Ann snoring away in their own rooms and he heard grunts come from downstairs where Brock sat in his armchair by the dying fire. At last Sam slipped softly from his bed and crept down. The Badger opened one eye and coughed.

'Now, Sam. You ought to be asleep. All that excitement has gone to your head,' said Brock.

'Brock,' cried Sam. 'I want to ask you something, Brock. I want to have a Fête of our own, without people or anything. Without any Vicar staring at me, and without any children, and nobody to say I'm ugly, and Ann's ugly. We aren't, are we, Brock?'

'No, Sam. Nothing to speak of. You are beautiful young pigs, all of you,' replied Brock, soothingly.

'Thank you, Brock,' said Sam. 'Well, can I have a Fête, all by myself, with your help?'

'Certainly, Sam. You've been to it, and you know all about it, so carry on, Sam,' said Brock, cheerfully.

Sam went back to bed and in a minute he was fast asleep.

The next day he was up very early and off to the fields before breakfast. He went to see Sally the Mare, and it was necessary to catch her before she began her day's work. She was eating her own breakfast of grass before going with the milkcart, and she looked surprised when little Sam scampered up to her.

'Oh, Sally,' panted Sam. 'Can you tell me where there's some bran? I want it for a bran tub, Sally. A bran tub.'

'There's plenty of bran in the barn, Sam,' said Sally. 'I'm sure Farmer Greensleeves will give you some if you ask him nicely.'

'Thank you, Sally,' said Sam. 'I can't stop now, but if you can come tonight and give away the prizes at our Fête, I shall be obliged.'

'What's that?' asked the astonished Mare. 'Prizes? Fête? Obliged? What do you mean, Sam?'

'Come to our woodland after you've done your work, Sally,' called Sam, running towards the farm and waving his hat as he vanished from sight.

He went to the barn, but the door was shut. He looked in at the dairy, and nobody was there. He peeped at the pigsty and the little pigs all leapt to their feet and squealed with joy.

'Here's Sam Pig come to play with us,' they cried.

'What's the matter with the pigs?' asked Farmer Greensleeves, who was in the cow-house, milking the cows.

He came to the door and saw little Sam.

'Hello. What do you want, Sam Pig? Have you come to help or to hinder?' he asked, but he laughed in a hearty way that made Sam feel happy.

'Please can I have some bran, Master Green-sleeves?' said Sam.

'What's it for?' asked the Farmer.

'For a bran tub,' said Sam. 'It's our Fête today.'

'Your Fête, is it? Go and help yourself, Sam Pig. It's in the big corn bin yonder.'

So Sam went to the barn and pushed open the lid of the great wooden bin, and propped it with a long rake. Then he dipped a wooden scoop in the bran and filled a sack.

He was just starting off with his burden when Farmer Greensleeves came in to see if he had closed the lid properly.

'Good, Sam. You've remembered to shut the lid and the door, but you've taken plenty of bran! You can hardly carry it. I'll put it on Sally's back and she can trot with you part way, but she must hurry back.'

'Oh, thank you, Master,' cried Sam.

The Farmer put the sack across Sally's back and told her to take it to the home of the four pigs and then to return at once.

Sally nodded her great head, and went off with Sam Pig riding her. Sam leaned down and opened the gates, and shut them after him. They went across the fields and the common and the wood to the secret little home where the animals lived.

'I'll take it now,' said Sam, when they reached an oak tree. 'I don't want the others to see it. Thank you very much, dear Sally.'

He took the sack off Sally's back and the Mare went home to her Master. She could press the latches of gates with her nose and close the gates after her, she was such a wise creature.

Sam rolled a little barrel from the woodshed and packed the bran into it, as he had seen the people do at the Fête.

'Now to magic it. Now to make nice things come into it,' said he, but although he wished and wished and waved a magic wand of hazel, and shook a white bluebell over it and dropped a four-leafed clover in it, nothing happened. It was bran and bran and bran.

'Sam. Where are you? Late again,' called Bill Pig, when Sam went in to breakfast. Everybody scolded him.

'Where have you been? Look at your dirty feet. You've been in the farmyard. You've been through a bog,' they cried, crossly.

'Did you get what you wanted?' asked Brock, serenely.

'Yes,' whispered Sam. 'I got it, but it isn't magical.'

'What isn't magical?' asked Tom and Bill.

'Bran, if you want to know,' said Sam, shortly.

'Of course it isn't,' said Tom, but little Ann suddenly knew what Sam was doing.

'Brock. It's the bran tub,' she whispered.

'Sh-sh-sh,' cried Sam. 'It's my secret, Ann. It's something nice for everybody.'

Brock stroked his nose and waited. He knew he must do something to help Sam.

'Get on with your breakfast, Sam,' said he, quietly.

'And mind you do all the washing up,' added Bill.

'And wiping, too,' said Tom.

After breakfast, when the little pigs were busy making beds, sweeping floors and shaking doormats, with Sam at the sink washing the pile of dishes, Brock took his bottle of magic from the top shelf of the kitchen and went out. Under the oak tree was the tub of bran, and Brock pushed his paw into it and shook it. Nothing was there except bran. He went into the wood and gathered several little objects – sticks and stones of curious shapes, herbs and berries. He sprinkled them with his lotion from the green bottle and tossed them in the tub. He stirred them round and shook the tub. Then he went back to the house.

'Leave the bran tub to me. Don't go near it,' said he to the little pig who was slowly wiping the plates without licking one of them. 'You get on with the other things and I'll look after the bran tub.'

'Will you magic it?' asked Sam, eagerly.

Brock nodded, and little Sam threw a plate up in the air and caught it as he shouted, 'Hurrah! Hurrah! Hurrah!'

Then he dropped the plate and it fell in fragments on the stone floor.

'Oh dear. I'm sorry, Brock,' said he. 'That's my spirits going up and down again.'

He gathered the fragments and put them in the corner, to be stuck together when Brock had taken some resin from the fir tree. That is the way they mended their china.

He scampered out to the green glade, a smooth piece of grass with trees around it. It was there he had once stood, a bewitched little pig, and he was always careful when he visited the place.

'This is where the Fête will be held,' he thought, and he took a piece of stick from his pocket and wrote:

TO THE FÊTE

in the sandy soil of the path. He wrote it with a charred stick on the silver birch tree and scribbled it on the trunk of the beech tree.

Then he ran home for the little bucket he used for his gardening, and he filled it with water from the spring. He dropped in a few green apples from the crab tree.

Near it he put a small bowl of flour from Tom's store.

He fetched the blanket from his bed and spread it on the ground for all to struggle under. He put a long stick across a bough for each pig to jump over.

He had no more barrels, so he could not arrange a row of empty barrels for the obstacle race, but he knew of a hollow tree through which they could pass.

There were no buns either, but there were pig-nuts and mushrooms and wild raspberries, which he heaped on the grass.

When all was ready he went back to look at the bran tub. He stared down at it, trying to look deep into it, but there was a notice saying: 'Don't touch.'

'I do hope it's magical,' said he. He stretched out his hand, but across the tub was a network of spiders' webs. He dare not push his arm through this. It was Brock's veil of secrecy. Away home he trotted, very content with the preparations.

'*Tom Pig, Bill Pig, Ann Pig and Brock,*
  Come to the Fête about three of the clock,' he sang.
'*Come in your best clothes, come at your leisure,*
  Dip in the bran tub and bring up a treasure.'

'Did you say a Fête?' asked Bill.

'Did you say a bran tub?' asked Tom.

'Did you say best clothes?' asked Brock.

'What is it in aid of?' asked Ann. 'It has to be in aid of something.'

'It's a Fête in aid of all the little-pigs-as-is-scolded-by-their-brothers-for-not-washing-up,' said Sam, quickly dodging away before his little pink ears were boxed.

'Where is it?' asked Tom.

'In the green glade,' said Sam.

'Where you were once a donkey,' laughed Bill.

But they all got ready, and dressed up for the grand occasion. Sam put on his hat, washed his face, stuck a feather in his hatband, and put a rose behind his ear and a straw in his mouth, to make himself very grown-up.

Then he took his position near the oak tree, at the entrance to the glade. He had a little box with a hole in it, and he held it up as each pig came forward.

'Walk up! Walk up! A penny for the Fête,' said he.

Ann dropped a pin into it, Tom and Bill dropped

buttons and Brock put something wrapped in a leaf. When Sam opened it he found a silver shilling from the money-box store.

'First I have much pleasure in calling on Mr Brock the Badger to open the Fête,' said Sam.

So Brock came forward and said a few words. 'Piglets and piglets and pigs of renown,' said he, bowing to right and to left, and little Ann made a deep curtsey in return.

'It gives me great pleasure to open this Fête in aid of one of your family who thinks he is put upon. It is a noble cause to help those little pigs-as-is-scolded-by-their-brothers-for-not-washing-up.'

They clapped their hands and Brock tossed a fistful of flower petals on the grass to show that the Fête was open.

They all walked round looking at the stalls. Sam had put flowers in one corner on the green moss, apples in another, fir cones in a third, and onions and potatoes in the fourth.

'Now for the egg-and-spoon race,' announced Sam. 'Please get ready for the egg-and-spoon race.'

'Where are the eggs and spoons?' asked Ann. 'Have you forgotten them, Sam?'

'Yes, I've forgotten them,' said Sam, crestfallen. Then he brightened. He picked a bunch of sycamore leaves and gave one to each pig.

'There's your spoon,' said he.

He reached up to a robin's nest and took out four

warm eggs. 'Excuse me,' said he to the bird, 'I'm only borrowing them.'

'Here are your eggs,' he said to his brothers and sister. 'Run quickly and don't break them, and then put them back in the nest.'

'Where shall we run?' asked the little pigs.

'Run round the oak tree, and round the beech tree and round the sycamore tree, and then put your eggs back in the nest. The first one wins the prize.'

'What prize?' asked Tom, suspiciously.

'Oh, I don't know. I can't think of everything. A prize,' cried Sam. 'Be quick or the eggs will get cold and the robin will be grieved.'

So away they scuttered, and they held their tiny eggs so carefully in the sycamore leaves that every egg was safely restored to the nest.

'Thank you. Thank you,' sang the Robin, who had been anxiously watching.

'Who won?' asked Bill.

'You all won,' said Sam. 'You'll all get prizes.'

The next was the three-legged race. Sam and Ann fastened their legs together, Tom and Bill fastened theirs, and Brock was the judge and whistle-blower.

They raced round the oak tree, the beech tree, the sycamore tree and all got in together.

'Who won?' asked Tom.

'You all won,' said Brock. 'You will all, I hope, get a prize.'

'I hope so, too,' said Sam, who was wondering

where all these prizes were coming from. He had forgotten the prizes.

The next race was the sack race, and Sam had also forgotten the sacks. Indeed, there was only the little sack which had held the bran.

Ann solved the difficulty. She ran home for the pudding bags in which pease puddings and dumplings were boiled. Each little pig draped a pudding bag over his head, and Brock tied the tapes. Then they all ran the race, but nobody won at all. They bumped into the trees, they fell in each other's arms, they tripped over stones, they rolled and laughed and kicked and fell until Brock had to untie all their heads.

'Brock the Badger won that race,' said Brock.

'Next is the obstacle race,' announced Sam, and he blew a loud whistle on his straw whistle pipe.

He showed them all the obstacles – the hollow tree through which they must scramble, the flour bag where they must dip their heads, the water bucket where the apples floated, the blanket under which they must crawl, the stick over which they must leap, the heap of corn and pig-nuts and mushrooms they must eat before they raced home to the oak tree.

Brock blew the whistle and off they went. They tried to scramble through the hollow tree, but Sam and Ann, Tom and Bill all stuck in the opening, and Brock had to pull them out and straighten them. Then they went to the flour bag to whiten their faces. How they laughed when they saw each other! They ducked for apples in the water bucket, and they crept under the blanket so quickly that they went along with the blanket on their four backs like some strange animal. They leaped over the stick. They gobbled up the heap of corn and pig-nuts, and they ran to the winning post. They all arrived together.

'Everybody's won. You've all got prizes,' cried Brock.

Then Sally the Mare came trotting up the lane.

'Am I too late?' she asked. 'I was ploughing and I couldn't come earlier.'

'You're just in time to dip in the bran tub with us,' said Brock, patting the Mare.

'Come along, everybody. Come and dip. Nothing for a dip,' he called, brushing away the cobwebs which protected the tub.

'Oh, I say, Brock, this is exciting,' cried Tom and Bill and Ann, but Sam said nothing. He was nervously wondering what was down in that bran tub.

Ann dipped first and brought out a fat, glossy chestnut made into a chair small enough for a fairy to sit upon. It had four long thorns in the back and four legs, with sheep's wool woven round to make the curving back and to hold the legs firm.

Tom dipped next and he brought out a little besom of green twigs from the silver birch. It was the neatest little besom you ever saw, tied together with silver ribbons made of cobwebs.

Bill thrust in his hand and he drew up a plum pudding made of nuts and barley, and cow-cake and turnips, all mixed in a ball, and tied in a pudding cloth.

'A pudding for all of us,' he called, and he threw it up and caught it.

Then Sam put in his hand and drew up a cage made of the white pith of rushes woven neatly, and inside was a peacock butterfly. The butterfly fluttered its lovely wings and Sam opened the door and let it fly away to the tree above their heads.

Then Sally dipped her nose in the tub, and she brought out a bundle of the sweetest hay.

'It's summer come today,' cried Sam, happily.

'Have another dip?' asked Brock. 'I don't think the bran tub is empty yet.'

So they all dipped again, with cries of joy.

Ann drew a box with a couple of glow-worms shining with a green light.

Tom drew out a cherry stone carved in the shape of a basket, with a glittering stone inside it, like a ruby.

Bill dipped low and found a green rush hamper with four white eggs from the farm.

Then Sally the Mare pushed her nose in the bran tub, and she brought out a bag with oats ready for enjoyment.

Lastly Sam dipped, and he found a leafy notebook, with a picture of a bird or a flower on each page.

Each flower gave out a sweet scent, each bird sang its own song. It was a book of magic and wonder and moonshine.

'Oh, Brock,' sighed Sam, in rapture. 'This is some of your very own magic.'

'Thank you. Thank you, Brock,' they all cried.

'Now I'll present the prizes,' said Sally the Mare.

'I forgot them,' sighed Sam.

'Never mind. I've a few prizes in my pockets,' said Brock. 'You have all won them so Sally must divide them.'

'Oh, Brock! You have saved me again,' whispered Sam.

Sally gave the peppermints, the barley sugar, the popcorn and the humbugs to the excited little pigs, with a fine gesture.

'I have great joy in presenting the prizes to four good friends of mine,' said she.

Then she went back to the farm, and Brock and the four little pigs went home.

'What a day!' said Sam. 'Oh, what a lovely Fête it has been and how happy I am.'

'What did we get for the little pigling-who-was-always-in-trouble?' asked Brock, his eyes twinkling.

'A silver shilling of Queen Elizabeth's time,' said Sam. 'I shall bore a hole in it and hang it on the wall to remind everybody.'

Sam Pig and the Steam-Roller

The country road was covered with sharp chippings of stone, which the roadman had spread over it. Carts bumped along, with rattling wheels and jolting passengers, and everyone who drove along this highway between the villages was shaken and bruised.

Little Sam Pig came out of the fields, wearing his check trousers and his big hat. He climbed through the hedge and stepped down on the rough road.

'My goodness! It is sharp and hurty,' he exclaimed, as he walked gingerly across to the low stone wall. 'The roadman has been mending it. Oh dear, I wish he'd leave it alone. I like the soft white dust, I like to lie down in it when nobody's looking, but this stony road is like a pin-cushion, all spikes and needles.'

Sam sat down on the low wall, a favourite resting place when the little Pig wanted to observe the passers-by. It was the wall where Robin-run-in-the-hedge grew, with ferns and toadflax and harebells for company. It was an ancient wall, smothered in a veil of many-coloured flowers, and very soft to sit upon, for the leaves and blossoms were like cushions.

So Sam sat upon this little wall, which divided the high road from the river, and he felt very content that he had crossed the stony way. He took a little brown notebook and a pencil from his pocket, as he had done before, for again he wanted to write about the things he saw. Once he could only make rough pictures, but now he knew his letters and he could write a few words.

He wrote about a cart which rattled past, the driver lurching to right and to left with the stones under the wheels. Then came the baker's van, and a motor car, and Sam wrote these words in his book, with his own spelling, and his own crooked letters.

There was a long silence, and nobody came. Sam listened to the river talking to itself, and he thought of the mermaid who lived in the green water and sometimes sat on the rocks in the middle of the rushing, foaming torrent. He was just going to try to find her, when there was a sound of a galloping horse, and a great clatter of wheels. Sam clung tightly to the wall, for he could see a cart coming very fast, bumping and swaying on the stones. To his amazement, he recognized Sally the Mare.

Sally tore past with Farmer Greensleeves tugging at the reins, shouting to her, 'Whoa, Sally! Whoa, old girl! Whoa! Steady now, Sally,' and Sally took no notice but raced on. She never looked at Sam, she ran so fast, and she disappeared round the corner before Sam could recover from the surprise.

'What's the matter with Sally?' Sam asked the river, but the river was too busy to speak. It whirled onwards, and the water hens swam across to the opposite bank, taking no notice of Sam or Sally.

Sam was going to slide off the wall to run after his friend when he remembered the sharp stones. He sat for a minute looking down at them with disgust. Then he heard a roaring, puffing sound in the distance.

'Oh dear! What's that? A dragon?' Sam wondered, uneasily. 'If it's the dragon come back, I know how to deal with it. I'm the dragon-tamer.'

His heart was beating fast, and he trembled a little, but he stayed on his perch. A puff of smoke came round the bend, and the roar increased. Then a green monster appeared, with heavy wheels and a funnel from which came clouds of black smoke. It was a steam-roller.

'Don't run away,' Sam warned himself. 'Be brave. Don't run.'

He sat there and watched the great thing come nearer. Then it stopped, and backed with a great roar, and much puffing; then onward it came, and the broad wheels flattened and rolled the stones with a scrunching noise.

'A good dragon,' murmured Sam, approvingly. 'It is making a nice road for Sally and for all the horses and carts and motors. The road was cruel sharp and now my feet won't be hurt.'

The steam-roller was a terrifying object, but it stayed on the road and made no effort to clamber on the wall, or to climb a tree. Two men were looking after it and when Sam spied their heads he dropped behind the wall and watched through a cranny. Men were more to be feared than steam-rollers and dragons.

So there he stayed, watching through the little hole, and the steam-roller went through its paces, backward and forward as it smoothed out the stony way.

After a time the men left the machine on the grassy verge and leaned for a smoke against the wall where Sam was hiding.

'Time to stop,' said one, looking at his watch. 'We'll leave her here.' They talked for a few minutes and then they covered up the steam-roller with a tarpaulin and went home.

Sam waited till all was quiet and then he came cautiously out, and lifted the cover. He examined the steam-roller but he said never a word, for the steam-roller seemed to be dozing. On the front was a little brass medallion of a prancing horse. It was just like Sally dancing on her hind-legs with fright.

He went to the farmhouse to inquire after the Mare. Sally was grazing in the meadow, but Sam could see by her uneasiness something had upset her.

'What's the matter, Sally?' asked Sam.

'Oh, Sam,' cried Sally, showing the whites of her eyes and flicking her ears nervously. 'I had such a fright. I met the steam-roller, that monster, and I ran away. I couldn't bear it.'

'But, Sally dear, surely you knew it wasn't a fierce beast?' asked Sam, gently stroking his friend.

'Yes, I knew that, but I ran away, Sam. It was my imagination. You have imagination, haven't you, Sam?'

Sam nodded.

'So have I,' Sally went on, 'and although I knew it was only the old steam-roller, yet I thought it might catch me. I thought I could hear it say, "I'll catch her. I'll catch her. Puff! Puff! Puff! I'll catch her." '

'It didn't mean it, Sally. It was only a joke, I'm sure,' said Sam, calming the excited Mare.

'Do go and have a talk with it, Sam,' said Sally. 'I expect it will listen to you. It likes to frighten horses, I'm sure. It wears the picture of one of us, rearing.'

'I'll have a chat with it,' said Sam. 'It's down by the side of the road, in that patch of grass where carts pass each other. It's covered with tarpaulin to keep it warm, as the men have gone home for the night. I'll talk to it.'

Sam went home to tea, and he told his family about the steam-roller that frightened Sally.

'Horses are nervous animals,' said Brock, slowly. 'They see more than most animals. They see ghosts, boggarts, and many creatures, and sometimes they know what is going to happen. They warn their drivers of danger. They feel it in the air.'

'I feel danger in the air sometimes,' said Sam, slyly glancing at Tom and Bill, who glowered back.

'I mean real danger,' said Brock. 'Horses and men talk together, and act together, so that a man on horseback is like the horse he rides and knows what will happen.'

'Then why did Sally run away?' asked Sam.

'If Farmer Greensleeves had been riding her, then she wouldn't have run away. He would have told her that the steam-roller was harmless,' said Brock.

'Well, I'm going to have a chat with the steam-roller,' said Sam. 'So long! Adieu! Goodbye!'

He darted off before anyone could say a word about washing up, and away he went across the fields to the highroad where the steam-roller was standing by the wall.

He climbed up on the back step and stoked the engine. There was a puff of smoke, and the engine began to work. Sam seized the lever and started off down the road.

When they came to a gate Sam sprang off and opened it. Then back he went and took the steam-roller inside the field. They went rollocky-rollocky over the grass, thumping and shaking, bumping and bruising, and a great curl of smoke came from the funnel and a great roar from the engine.

'Where are you taking me, Sam Pig?' groaned the steam-roller. 'This shakes my vitals.'

'I'm taking you home to the four pigs and Brock the Badger,' said Sam.

'It's beyond my powers,' said the steam-roller. 'I can never get there, all across this uneven ground.'

'Keep going,' commanded Sam, and away they went, roaring like a lion. They broke down bushes and pushed through hedges, and made a trail across the grass.

At last with a deep groan the engine stopped.

'Can't do it, Sam! Can't do it! Here I be and here I stay,' cried the steam-roller.

'Poor thing,' said Sam, climbing down and patting its side. 'I'll fetch Brock the Badger and my family to see you. Wait here for me.'

'I have to wait, Sam. I can't move any more,' said the steam-roller sadly.

Sam ran home for his family. 'There's the steam-roller out in the field,' said he. 'I was bringing it home, but it can't go any further.'

Brock hurried out, with the little pigs following him.

'Stupid, Sam! Fancy bringing the steam-roller here,' cried Tom.

'It's a good thing it broke down, Sam,' said Brock, crossly. 'You'll have Man coming after it and finding our house. Whatever made you bring such a thing as a steam-roller out here in the fields and woods?'

'I wanted to try to tame it,' said Sam. 'I wanted it not to frighten horses any more.'

The steam-roller looked very dejected in the middle of the field. Sally the Mare pranced up and down the next field in a fright, so Sam ran to fetch her, too.

'Come along, Sally, I want you to meet the steam-roller. It can't move now,' said Sam.

Sally nervously followed Sam, but when she saw the steam-roller standing so sadly in the flowery meadow, she lost her fears.

'Oh, you poor thing,' said she. 'Can't you get away?'

'No, I'm stuck!' said the steam-roller, and a tear fell with a splash on the ground. 'Sam has brought me here, away from the road where I live, and goodness knows how I shall ever get back.'

'Let's make the best of it,' said Brock. 'We'll have supper out here and a little party with you as our guest, if you will accept our hospitality, steam-roller.'

'Thank you,' replied the steam-roller, so dolefully that it made Sally and Sam laugh.

Sally came very close and rubbed her nose on the funnel, smelling the smooth green-painted metal. Then Sam fetched a few eggs and a frying pan and he cooked them on the fire. Bill gave the steam-roller a drink of water, and Sally drank from the same bucket. Ann boiled a kettle and made a cup of tea. Tom ran home for some cake and a few carrots and apples.

The steam-roller didn't care for such food, but it enjoyed the sticks Ann threw on its fire and the water Bill gave it. Sally ate the apples and carrots, and Tom and Bill ate the cake.

'Tell us a story, Steam-roller,' begged Sam, and Sally the Mare, who had completely lost her fear, said she too would like to hear a tale from the steam-roller.

'Once upon a time,' began the steam-roller, 'when I was very young, I was taken to the Big House to level the drive. I was going up and down, puffing with a great noise, when I saw a little red fox running through the trees. It came towards me, and then it leaped high and sat on my arm. The men who were looking after me said nothing, but the hunt came down the drive. I let out a roar and the horses all swerved aside, and nobody saw that fox sitting there. Then the hunt went on, and the little fox stayed with me all morning, warming its toes, and enjoying itself. When the men went home, the fox crept out and thanked me. Then it went safely back to its den.'

'That was a nice tale, Steam-roller,' said Ann. So she told the tale of Cinderella, but the steam-roller thought she had told it all wrong.

'I heard that Cinderella went to the ball on a steam-roller,' said the steam-roller, puffing out a curl of smoke.

'Oh no, it was a coach and six, made out of a pumpkin and six mice,' Ann assured it. The steam-roller shook its head.

Then the steam-roller asked a riddle.

'What is most like a horse frightened of a steam-roller?' it asked.

The little pigs tried and tried, but they couldn't find the answer.

'A mare, of course,' said the steam-roller, proudly.

Sam asked a riddle, too, and he begged his brothers not to tell the answer.

'What makes more noise than a pig squealing under a gate?'

The steam-roller suggested that it always made much more noise than a pig squealing under a gate, but Sam shook his head. It wasn't the right answer. At last he told the steam-roller.

'What makes more noise than a pig squealing under a gate? Why, two pigs squealing under a gate.'

The steam-roller didn't laugh. It couldn't see the joke, and it never would see it, so they gave up asking riddles.

The steam-roller had no sense of humour, they decided, and they were very sorry for the great cumbrous thing.

Brock stood near and he puffed his pipe until a cloud came out as big as the steam-roller's smoke.

'I want to go back,' said the steam-roller. 'My place is on the roads, not out here in the fields. Your Sam brought me, and he should take me back.'

'I'll fetch a drop of my powerful oil,' said Brock. 'It will cure your trouble and Sam must take you where you belong. He ought not to have come here with you.'

Brock went home for his green bottle from the top shelf, and the little pigs clambered on the steam-roller and enjoyed themselves. Ann made a garland of purple vetch to go about the tall green neck of the steam-roller. Bill hung a few parsnips on the boiler and Tom put a bunch of onions on the spokes of the wheels. Sam fetched his paint box and made another picture instead of the prancing rearing horse. He made a little picture of a smiling pig offering the

steam-roller a bunch of carrots and he hung it on the funnel. Luckily the steam-roller didn't see it, or it might have been offended.

Then Brock came back with the oil, which he poured in the steam-roller's veins. Immediately the creature let out a roar and a whistle and began to prance. Sam sprang to the step and away they went across the fields, through hedges, and over ditches, back to the highroad.

Then Sam covered the panting, trembling steam-roller with the tarpaulin, and said good night.

'Good night, Sam,' said the steam-roller, in a small voice.

'I hope you are all right,' said Sam, anxiously peeping under the cloth.

'Oh yes, only a bit shaken,' stammered the steam-roller. 'Go away, Sam Pig. Leave me to go to sleep. That medicine Brock gave me was very strong.'

'Good night,' said Sam. 'You won't frighten Sally again, will you?'

'No, I promise,' sighed the steam-roller. 'I doubt if I shall ever frighten anyone.'

So Sam left it to sleep.

The next day when the roadmen came they were much surprised to find the steam-roller with a garland round its funnel and onions and parsnips adorning its wheels, and most of all they stared at the little picture of a dancing pig where the prancing horse ought to be.

'Strange doings!' said the men. 'Look at the dirt on the wheels. There's the track through that gateway. What's been on in the night?'

But although they inquired if anyone had seen a steam-roller careering about, nobody knew anything about it.

Sam Pig and the Jack-in-the-Green

In the village every May Day there were processions and garlands and merry makings to welcome in the Spring. The farmers decorated their horses with ribbons and flowers, and tassels of straw on their manes. The cows frisked in the pastures, the lambs danced and ran races, and the children had a holiday from school.

A Jack-in-the-Green came skipping up the village streets, with all the children following him, and the people stood on the pavements talking and laughing at his antics. It was an ancient custom, they told the strangers who sometimes joined in the sport. It was something remembered from long past days.

May Day was the loveliest day in all the year, when the Maypole was set up in the field, and a band played, while little boys and girls each holding a coloured ribbon tripped around it in orderly fashion so that the ribbons made a pattern as they wound themselves about the pole.

Once, as you remember, Sam and Ann joined them in this sport, and they had seen the Queen of the May.

It was the day when everybody went out to gather branches of may blossom to deck their front doors and their door posts. Young girls caught the dew in their hands and washed their faces to make themselves beautiful. Ann Pig always went out at dawn on May Day to collect dew, but although she washed herself till her face shone, nobody could truthfully say she was beautiful.

On May Day there was excitement in the house of the four pigs and Brock the Badger, for Brock kept a note of the day, and they made grand preparations for the festival.

'Human beings forget these things,' Brock told his friends. 'They don't all gather may nowadays, and they go to work with solemn faces. They shake their heads and sing doleful songs. They forget, but I'm glad to say the children remember, because their mothers tell them about it, and they run out and gather may and have their holidays and feasts. But we animals remember always.'

Sam and Ann went out at dawn with the garden wheelbarrow and picked great bunches of shining may blossom. There were buds round as pearls, and flowers flecked with crimson, and leaves in dainty clusters, for the may blossom grows in bunches ready for a garland, a bouquet, a buttonhole. As for the scent of it, the little pigs wrinkled their noses and sniffed and sniffed with delight.

'I should like to put it in a bottle and keep it all

the year. I should like to smell it at Christmas,' said Ann Pig.

'Someday I'll try my skill, little Ann,' Brock promised her. 'I'll try to put the scent in a bottle and keep it for you, but not now, I'm busy.'

'I don't want scent,' said Sam Pig. 'That's for girls. I likes the smell of bracken and trees and moss and dirt and farmyards and cows and horses and . . .'

'Come and decorate before breakfast,' said Brock, interrupting his flow. 'We must have everything fine for May morning.'

They made garlands and hung them on the door, and they sprinkled may blossom on the kitchen floor for a scented carpet. They pinned bunches of may at the windows to flutter with the clean white curtains, and they fastened branches across the oak beam of the roof, so that the tiny house looked as if it were a real live may tree growing there.

Then they sat down to breakfast, with new-laid eggs and cream and porridge, and snowy bread, and a dish of hawthorn leaves for a salad.

They talked of the festivities in the village and all wished they could see the sights.

'Brock,' said Sam, suddenly. 'Brock. Will you take us to see the Jack-in-the-Green?'

'There will be many people in the village,' said Brock. 'I don't want my four little pigs to be captured.'

'If we go quietly they won't see us,' said Ann. 'I

should wear my flowery hat and we should be very good.'

'Yes, we would be as good as . . . as . . . Sally,' added Sam.

'I think it would be better if you went with Farmer Greensleeves,' said Brock. 'I might go by myself, for I can pass unnoticed, but you ought to have someone with you. He may be taking his children.'

'He is,' cried Sam, excitedly. 'Sally told me. She is having her shoes blacked and her coat brushed and her mane plaited and bells hung on her harness. The cart was washed yesterday, and I helped to polish the wheels.'

'But Farmer Greensleeves may not want us,' said Ann, sadly. 'Do you think he will, Sam?'

'I don't know,' said Sam, doubtfully. 'There's a lot of us, and Mrs Greensleeves will say, "There come those bothersome little pigs again. We haven't room for them in the cart." '

'It's early yet,' said Brock. 'We got up at dawn. It's only six o'clock in the morning. There's plenty of time. You can run over to the farm and ask Sally. She will be in the stable all decorated, I expect, Sam.'

'Yes,' said Sam. 'I'll go. Sally's mane and tail were plaited last night, and this morning the farmboy will untie her hair and it will be curly like my tail.'

Sam went off to the farmhouse, gathering flowers on the way, to add his own to Sally's adornment.

Sally stood in the stable, eating sweet hay from the

manger and drinking from a bucket of sparkling water from the spring. Her hair was curly, her shoes were blacked, and her tail was twined with ribbons down the centre with the rest flowing loose.

Farmer Greensleeves and his family were having breakfast when Sam arrived, and nobody was about. Sam went across the yard on tiptoes, lest anyone should hear him.

'Sally? Are you there?' he whispered.

The Mare turned her head, and pricked her ears. Sam climbed up to unbolt the bottom half of the door. Then he went in the warm dark stable, with its brushes, its stool and manger.

'A Happy May Day,' said he, holding out a bouquet of may blossom, bluebells and violets he had picked.

'A Happy May Day,' returned Sally.

'Are you going to the village?' asked Sam.

'Yes, of course. I always take the family on May Day to see the Jack-in-the-Green,' said Sally, happily munching the hay. 'After I've taken the milk to the station I shall have the extra decorations on me, and then away we shall go.'

Sam looked at the ground. He kicked a bucket, and frowned. Sally wondered what was the matter.

'Have you put up your may boughs, Sam?' she asked.

'Yes. We've put up some and Tom and Bill and Ann are finishing off now.'

'What is it, Sam?' asked Sally, quietly.

'We all want to see the Jack-in-the-Green,' said Sam. 'We want to go with Farmer Greensleeves. Do you think he will take us?'

'Not in the cart, Sam. There wouldn't be room. Missis wouldn't like to go with a load of pigs on May Day,' said Sally, shaking her head sadly. 'But maybe Master would keep an eye on you there, if you went by yourselves. Ask him, Sam.'

There was a sound of doors opening and little Sam slipped away to the stack-yard to wait his chance. The milk cart went off with the morning's milk and Sam waited. He crept close to a haystack, pulled the hay over his face and went to sleep.

The cart returned, and the bustle began, so that Sam awoke and hid himself until there was a chance to speak to the Farmer without Mrs Greensleeves seeing him and sending him away.

The best cart was brought out to the farmyard and the two children decorated it with branches of may, with bunches of bluebells and the first roses. Farmer Greensleeves twined blue and yellow ribbons in Sally's mane and the farmboy brushed and polished her shoes again. The best harness was brought out with the bells and ornaments of brass, with white tassels and horse-brasses to hang on Sally's face.

Sam Pig came creeping nearer and nearer, and at last he could resist no longer.

'Farmer Greensleeves! Master!' he said, and the Farmer looked round in surprise.

'Why, Sam Pig! What are you doing here? A Happy May Day.'

'Same to you, Master,' replied Sam. 'I was wondering if you would let us stand near you in the village, when the Jack-in-the-Green goes past. We all want to see it, and Brock won't let us go alone.'

'Certainly, Sam. I took you to the circus and you were well-behaved. Only that time when I took you to market and you went and helped yourself to ribbons was I ashamed of you.'

'Yes, Master,' murmured Sam.

'But Missis won't like to be seen with a drove of pigs, Sam. You must dress up nicely and keep back, and keep quiet, too. Don't talk, don't squeak, and don't push. Promise?'

'I promise, Master,' said Sam, eagerly. 'Thank you very much. We'll carry boughs of may blossom, and nobody will notice us, so long as we are near you.'

Mrs Greensleeves was coming across the yard, and her quick eye spied Sam.

'There's that pigling again. Off you go, Sam!' she cried, clapping her hands and shooing Sam away, and off he went, with just one backward look and a grin at Sally.

'Meet you at the Jack-in-the-Green,' called Mr Greensleeves.

'What, meet those pigs? Never!' cried Mrs Green-sleeves, but her husband laughed at her fears.

'They are only young, and Sam is a friend of mine and of Sally's. He helped with the haymaking, my dear.'

Sam went home with the good news, and the family washed themselves and dressed in their best clothes. They gathered branches of may blossom to carry, and they wore garlands of spring flowers round their necks – primroses and purple orchids, goldilocks and birds'-eye.

'We shall look like part of the May Day Show,' said Ann, as she sniffed at the bluebells and prim-roses.

'Oh, I am so happy,' cried Sam. 'I wish you were going, Brock.'

'I shall go, Sam, but you won't see me, for I shall keep away from your party,' said Brock, who looked exactly like an old farm labourer with his pipe and his coat and his stick.

'Tell us about Jack-in-the-Green,' said Sam, as they all stood ready to start on their journey.

Brock nodded. 'Sit down for a while,' said he; and they perched themselves on stones in the garden and listened to his words, for they were curious about the Jack and his green bower of leaves.

'You will see a dancing man, embowered in leaves, so that you can't see his face or body. You might think he was a tree dancing up the village, for he will be hidden in a framework of greenery. They call him Jack-in-the-Green, and some of the children will run after him, singing and waving flowers and flags.'

'Oh, I do want to see him,' cried Ann.

'Like a bower of leaves, dancing up the road,' said Sam. 'I'm so glad we are going.'

'The village folk think he is their own Jack, but they are wrong. He belongs to the woods, and he is as old as time itself. He goes back to the ancient days when we badgers were free to wander the earth, and to have great stretches of country for our very own. He was once the god of the woodlands, and we knew him. Every animal is a Jack-in-the-Green, because we hide in the green bushes, and peep through them to see who is coming and where danger lies.'

'I should like to meet Jack-in-the-Green,' said Sam.

'What is he really like? Like a human being or an animal?' asked Tom.

'Neither, Tom,' said Brock, slowly. 'He's really a spirit of the woods, sacred to the earth, and we animals bow down before him. We can see him, but men cannot. Yet he seldom appears, only in times of danger, or when he wants us to view him. That is the real Jack-in-the-Green. The figure you will see at the village is a picture in a way, to remind all of us, villagers and animals and all, of the spirit of the woods who dances invisible and all-powerful, in leafy ways.'

They all sat very quietly listening, for Brock's face

was suddenly solemn as he recalled the ancient wisdom of the woods, the things men had forgotten.

Then Brock smiled, and sprang to his feet.

'Off you go,' he cried. 'Enjoy yourselves. I shall be somewhere about.'

They went across the green lanes, by the long-forgotten tracks, over little streams, on the slopes of the hills, and then they dipped down to the valley. The farm cart had to come by the valley roads and the little pigs kept a look-out for Sally. They walked close together, with their garlands and nosegays, and they looked like a bunch of small children going to the fair.

When Sally trotted past them Mrs Greensleeves smiled down at them, and the Farmer and the children waved. They were already near the village for they could hear the band playing.

'Is my hat straight?' asked Ann.

'Do I look like a boy?' asked Sam.

They held their bouquets close to their faces, and went on, past the little cottages and the mill, past the village shop and Post Office to the market place.

They could see Sally, tied to an iron ring in a wall, and then they spied Farmer Greensleeves, who was looking for them. Already the crowd lined the village street and the little pigs kept close to the walls, as they went softly towards the beckoning Farmer.

'Keep near me,' he whispered. 'You're all right. I've kept a good place for you.'

They stood in front of Farmer Greensleeves, close to his legs, with their garlands and flowers and necklaces, like a company of players.

'You are grand,' said the Farmer, laughing. 'People will want you to join the mummers down the street.'

The pipes tootled an air, the drum rolled, the fiddle squealed, and the band moved along the street. Then came the Jack-in-the-Green, like a whirling bower of leaves, with ribbons and flowers tucked in the greenery.

Everyone cheered, and children ran out to join the procession. Sam Pig and Ann, Tom Pig and Bill, all clapped their hands, and whispered happily. They must not go among the rest, they knew, and they stared enchanted at the lovely scene.

Then, to everyone's surprise, there was a movement in the distance, and another Jack-in-the-Green came twisting and dancing down the street. Another bower of leaves whirled around with scarlet and gold ribbons, and strange little flowers in the greenery. Music came from it, the Jack-in-the-Green was playing his own pipes, and the sweetness and wildness of the tune made people's feet begin to dance, so that in a minute everyone was jigging up and down, laughing merrily.

'Another Jack ... Another Jack. Where has he come from? Can't he dance! He dances better than the first Jack,' they said.

Two bright eyes looked out from the bower, but

nothing else could be seen as the figure whirled past, playing the enchanting tune, which seemed to bring all the joys of earth back to life again.

Sam stared, for he had caught a glance from those shining eyes. He knew them. It was Brock the Badger, but somehow Brock was different. He said nothing, for the others hadn't recognized him.

'That's a wonderful sight,' said Farmer Greensleeves, slapping his knees and clapping his hands in time to the music. 'In all my born days I've never seen such a Jack-in-the-Green as that one. You're lucky to be here today, Sam. I wonder where he comes from?'

'From the wild woods, I think,' murmured Sam.

'Maybe. He's not like any dancer I've ever seen,' said the Farmer. 'They say . . . they say . . .'

'What do they say?' whispered Mrs Greensleeves.

'They say the real Jack-in-the-Green comes back once in a hundred years.'

The music died away in the distance and the crowd moved forward to see the new Jack. The first Jack-in-the-Green was resting at the door of the Inn. He put his red face out of the wicker bower of leaves and sipped a tankard of ale.

When the second dancer arrived, he held out the tankard and called to him.

'Come along, Jack-in-the-Green. Show thyself,' said he. 'We didn't expect company. Two Jacks at the May Day!'

But the second Jack-in-the-Green danced on, twirling faster than ever, and the music of his pipes grew wilder and more beautiful. Away he danced, out of the square, out of the village, and away towards a wood. After him ran the children and some of the men. When they got to the trees the Jack had disappeared completely. He had faded away as if he had gone down into the ground. Only the bower of leaves lay there, with the strange ribbons and laces of gold and green, and the flowers.

From one to another the word passed. 'The real Jack-in-the-Green has come back today,' said the old people. 'He will bring us good luck. We shall have good crops this year, and prosperity in the harvest. The ancient Jack has come to this village of ours.'

The little pigs stayed to see the fun in the market place and Farmer Greensleeves bought each of them a bag of brandy-snaps and May Day comfits and cakes.

'You've all been on your best behaviour,' he told them. 'I'll take you somewhere else one of these days. Nobody can say you don't behave well when you want.'

'I agree,' said Mrs Greensleeves graciously. 'It has been a lovely May Day, and you look very nice with your flowers.'

'You'd best go home and not stay for the maypole dance,' said Farmer Greensleeves. 'That old Jack-in-the-Green went dancing down your way. Perhaps you will see him in the woods.'

'Goodbye, Master. Thank you very much for letting us come to the Jack-in-the-Green,' piped little Sam Pig, and Ann curtseyed in her best manner, and the others bowed low.

Then away they went home, over the fields and woods, across the brooks and streams by stepping stones. By the side of the wildest little stream, just where the yellow broom hung over the water in a fountain of yellow flowers, sat Brock the Badger. He held a reed whistle-pipe to his lips and he was playing a tune they recognized.

'That's the tune the Jack-in-the-Green played,'

said Ann. 'Brock, there were two Jacks, and the second one played just like you. He danced better nor the first. He was lovely. Oh, yes! I liked him.'

'Did you see him?' asked Brock, with a twinkle.

'No, he was hidden in the leaves, but I liked him, Brock,' said little Ann, solemnly.

'So did we,' said Tom and Bill.

'What about you, Sam? Did you like the second Jack-in-the-Green?' asked Brock.

'I liked him as much as I like Brock the Badger,' said Sam, firmly, and he and Brock smiled together secretly.

The Hole in the Trousers

Little Sam Pig had a good voice, and sometimes he sang instead of talking. He felt that he was like the birds, who always whistle and sing to one another. Tom and Bill scolded him when he sang too much. He made their teeth ache, they said. He sang like a saw cutting a tree, or a creaking wagon going downhill, or like a little pig under a gate.

Now Sister Ann was different. She too was a singer, and she always replied in singing when Sam began.

One day Sam found a hole in his trousers, and he called Ann's attention to it. Ann was the mender, the sewer, the seamstress, the knitter. It was quite right to tell Ann, but on this particular day Ann didn't want to sew. She was out enjoying the sunshine, smelling the flowers, watching the birds.

Sam began like this: and anyone else can sing his song.

'*There's a hole in my trousers, my trousers, my trousers.*
There's a hole in my trousers, Sister Ann, Sister Ann.'

Ann replied in her clear high voice:

'Take a needle and mend it, and mend it, and mend it.
Take a needle and mend it, my lazy young Sam.'

Sam went on:

'Where's the needle to mend it, to stitch it, to mend it?
Where's the needle to mend it, O dear Sister Ann?'

Ann laughed and told her brother:

'There's a needle on the thorn bush, the whin bush, the
    gorse bush.
There's a needle on the thorn bush, O lazy young Sam.'

Then Sam asked:

'But how shall I patch it, and patch it, and patch it?
But how shall I patch it, O sweet Sister Ann?'

Ann replied:

'There's a patch in the cabbage, the cabbage, the cab-
    bage.
There's a patch in the cabbage, O dear Brother Sam.'

Then Sam asked:

'Oh, where is the cotton, the cotton, the cotton?
The cotton to mend it, O dear Sister Ann?'

Ann replied:

'Use yonder fine cobweb, fine cobweb, fine cobweb.
With yonder fine cobweb you can sew it, young Sam.'

Sam asked again:

'Oh, where is the thimble, a brass or gold thimble,
A new or old thimble, my dear Sister Ann?'

Ann replied:

> 'In yonder tall nut tree, tall nut tree, tall nut tree.
> In yonder tall nut tree, my small Brother Sam.'

Sam told her:

> 'But I cannot climb it, not climb it, not climb it.
> But I cannot climb it, dear Sister Ann.'

Ann replied:

> 'Oh, then you must shake it, must shake it, must shake
> it.
> Oh, then you must shake it, my dear little Sam.'

Then Sam went to the nut tree and shook it. Showers of nuts fell down on the little pig's head and he sang:

> 'Then down came the walnuts, the cobnuts, the filberts.
> Down came the big nuts, the small nuts for Sam.'

So Sam took a nutshell and put it on his finger for a thimble. He took a needle from the thorn bush, and some cotton from the cobweb. He found a patch in the cabbages and then he sewed the hole in his trousers.

He sang again:

> 'My trousers are mended, my beautiful trousers.
> A cabbage has patched them, my dear Sister Ann.'

Ann replied:

> 'I'm sure that I never knew you were so clever,
> You're exceedingly clever, my dear little Sam.'

So Sam kicked up his heels and ran off to sing the song to Sally the Mare.

Sam Pig Visits Primrose Cottage

In the lane near the Farm stood an ancient thatched cottage, with a well in the garden and a honeysuckle over the porch. Sam often loitered by the gate, looking in at the flowers and fruit, longing to pick a few strawberries, or a juicy carrot. Sometimes he saw old Mrs Dobbie in her white apron and sunbonnet of lilac print.

One day the furniture was taken away in a cart and the old lady went to live with her daughter.

Sam noticed that the curtains had gone from the window, and as the days passed the cottage had a neglected air. The gate was broken, the roses straggled over the path, and weeds grew high.

One evening Sam ventured up the garden path, between the lavender bushes which stood on guard, like aged grey men. He pushed at the door and it came open. He stepped inside the little house with a gasp of delight.

'A house of my own,' said he. 'I've always wanted to live alone, without Tom and Bill bothering me. Once I lived in a hole-in-the-road, but the Policeman turned me out. That was a nice house. I invited Tom and Bill and Ann to join me there, but I'll keep this house to myself.'

He scampered upstairs and down, counting the rooms. 'Four rooms, or is it five?' he asked himself, and he counted again and again. One bedroom and another opening out of it, one kitchen and a parlour.

'Four rooms! A palace,' murmured Sam. 'One room for Sam, one for Ann, one for Bill and one for Tom, but none for Brock the Badger. Then I won't invite them. I'll live here all alone.'

He looked in the cupboard in the kitchen and found a morsel of candle and a box of matches. Nothing else was in the house, nothing to eat at all.

'I'll go off to the Farm and see what I can get,' thought he. 'I won't go home, or they might find out.'

He ran off to the farmyard and brought back an empty sack and a bundle of straw which the thatcher had left.

'A fine bed,' said he, 'the best straw mattress.'

Then he returned and hunted under the edge of the haystack where the straying hen often laid her eggs. Two brown eggs lay there, and he felt very content as he carried them off. He had a piece of bread and cheese in his pocket, so there was a good supper, with a lettuce from the garden, and a carrot or two.

He went upstairs to the front bedroom, whose window overlooked the garden and lane.

'I'll sleep here,' said he. He spread the straw mat-

tress on the floor and sat down to eat his supper. It tasted excellent, and he sang a little song, and danced a jig, before he settled down for the night.

> *'Here am I,*
> *All alone,*
> *In a nice little cottage*
> *I call my own.'*

The moon was shining in at the window when he had finished and he opened the sash and listened to a nightingale singing in the lane. Then he lay down to sleep.

'Whoo-oo-oo,' cried a ghostly voice, and Sam sat up with his hair on end.

'Whoo-oo-oo,' screeched the voice again, and Sam cried, 'Who's there?'

An owl flew in at the open window and circled the room with snowy wings. It perched on the mantelpiece, and stared so hard with great unwinking eyes that Sam shivered.

'What are you doing in my house?' asked the owl.

'This is my house,' said Sam. 'I found it.'

'No, it is my house, Sam Pig, so you must move to another room,' hooted the owl and it suddenly darted at Sam and tweeked his ear so that he let out a cry of terror.

Sam took up his mattress and ran to the second bedroom. He banged the door, and mopped his forehead, and then he spread the bed on the floor and lay down to sleep. This was a smaller room and the floor was broken, and at the window tapped a rose-tree.

'Tap, tap, tap,' went the rose-tree, pushing its stalks through the pane. 'This is my house, Sam Pig.'

'Go away,' muttered Sam. 'I'm tired. Go away.'

He shut his eyes and began to think of the family.

'They'll wonder where I am,' he chuckled. 'Tom will be sorry he grumbled at me this morning. Bill will be sorry he cuffed me. Ann will be sorry, although she is always kind. Brock will go hunting but he'll never find me.'

He was just dozing off when there was a scuffle and a rustle and something ran over his face. Then a soft tail tickled his ear, and something furry sat on his nose.

Sam sneezed, and rolled over, flinging out his arms.

'Squeak, squeak,' cried the little mice, and they raced backward and forward over the fat little body of the sleepy pigling.

'Stop!' cried Sam. 'Stop! This is my house! It's all my house except for the next room where the owl lives.'

'No,' cried the mice. 'This is our house now Mrs Dobbie has gone. She gave it to us. She always fed us with bread and cheese. She kept a cat, and we dodged it, but now the cat has gone and we have the house all to ourselves.'

'It's my house, I found it,' cried Sam, indignantly.

'No, it's our home, our nursery and playground – except the next room where the owl lives.'

'Do you know who I am?' asked Sam sternly.

'No,' laughed the mice, 'nor do we care.'

'I am Sam Pig! I once saved Jemima Mouse from a trap,' said Sam importantly. 'I kept her in my pocket, and visited her house in a shoe where she lived.'

'Oh, Jemima: she's our great-grandmother! We don't care a straw for old Jemima. We are young and frolicsome,' cried the mice and they danced and pirouetted and tickled Sam's nose and pulled his tail and dragged at his ears until he had to stand up.

'Let's play rounders,' said the mice, chasing noisily round the room.

Sam stared at their game, as they threw a tiny ball, made from a robin's pin-cushion, to one another.

'I've never seen such a rowdy lot,' grumbled Sam.

'Let's waltz,' cried the mice, and they spun round to the music of the nightingale in the lane outside.

'I'm going downstairs,' said Sam, crossly. 'There's no peace in this room. No wonder the old lady left. I should like to bring Brock the Badger here. Why doesn't the owl eat you all?'

'He's afraid,' said the noisy little mice, spinning up and down. Peals of laughter followed Sam as he stumped down the narrow winding stair, and when he fell over the uneven steps and rolled to the bottom the mice squealed with joy.

Sam settled down in the parlour, but he could hear the patter of feet overhead and the noise of the mice crying, 'How's that! How's that, umpire?'

'I do believe they are playing cricket,' muttered Sam, dragging the sack half over his head. 'I never knew mice could be like this.'

At last he fell asleep, but he was awakened by something flipping over his face, beating him with faint blows like breaths of wind.

'What's that? What's that?' he cried, uneasily.

By the light of the moon he could see a company of bit bats flittering round the room, flying silently until they came close to him, when they dived at his head.

'Bit bats, get out of here,' cried Sam, shaking his fist at them. 'This is my house. I'm going to live here.'

'No,' cried the bats, with shrill squeaks. 'No. This is our house. We've been living under the thatch for many a year. Now the old woman has gone we have taken the house for ourselves, our children and our grandchildren. It's ours.'

'I won't budge,' said Sam, crossly. 'I'm bigger than you.'

'You can't fly,' cried the bats, circling round his head and tormenting him with their fine claws and their leathery wings.

They swooped at his nose, they darted and squealed, till at last Sam had to give in.

'Keep your room,' said Sam. 'I'm going to the kitchen.'

He dragged his bag of straw behind him and pushed open the kitchen door. It was comfortable and homely, and he gave a sigh of relief. He spread the mattress before the fireplace and settled down. There were no owls or mice or bats to be seen, and although he could hear thuds and squeaks in the distance he knew the creatures were too busy playing their night games to bother with him.

He shut his eyes and went to sleep. He had only been asleep for a few minutes when he heard footsteps coming up to the front door. He sat up in alarm. This was some large animal. Perhaps it was a bear or a wolf coming to eat him up.

There was silence and then a shuffling sound at the door. It was pushed open and something entered the parlour. Sam made a rush for the cupboard and shut the door after him. He moved silently as Brock had taught him in times of danger, for here was real danger as he knew very well. Everything was silent. The owl stopped hooting, the mice went to their holes, the bats hung down by their feet and all was still as they listened to their enemy.

The kitchen door moved, very slowly, and Sam held his breath in terror. There was a bang and a thump as a bag was thrown on the ground, and a gruff voice spoke.

'Anyone here? Ah, I'm dead beat! I'm glad to find this place. I'll doss off for a bit till it's pitch dark.'

The man stumbled over the little mattress and kicked it aside. 'Somebody has been here. Well, I'll kill him if he comes back. I'm here now.'

He grunted and sighed and coughed and moaned, and choked and grumbled. Then he lay down and took off his boots and threw them with a clatter across the room. He struck a match and lit his pipe. Sam watched him through a crack in the cupboard door and he shivered as he saw the evil face.

The man smoked his pipe and then lay down. In a minute he was snoring.

Sam crept to the cupboard door but he couldn't escape without disturbing the heavy boots which lay there. He moved silently, pushing gently, but after a time the man awoke and sat up. The church clock was striking twelve. The man arose, put on his boots, and laced them up. He emptied the straw from Sam's sack. Then he slipped a pair of gloves on his hands and a pair of thick socks over his boots. Like a ghost he went to the door and out into the darkness with the sack under his arm.

'In ten minutes I shall bag them all,' he muttered.

Sam scrambled out of the cupboard and followed him. 'I won't let him go to our farm,' thought Sam. 'I'll see what he is going to do.'

The man walked softly down the path and Sam rushed upstairs to fetch the mice and the owl.

'There's a man going to rob the Farmhouse,' cried Sam. 'Come and help me.'

Then down he ran, followed by a drove of mice and a white-winged owl. The bats joined him as he went out to the garden and away after the man they hurried. He was walking very softly up the lane, across the field to the Farmhouse and Sam and his companions went too.

The owl and the bats flew overhead, but the man never saw them. The mice ran alongside and their faint rustle was lost in the grasses. Sam trotted silently behind.

Into the farmyard went the man, but he turned away from the house as if he knew Roger the house-dog was there. Instead, he crossed the stackyard and went towards the hen-house.

'He's going to rob the hen-roost,' said Sam to himself, as the man twisted a wire in the lock and then forced the door.

'Quick, all of you! At him! At him!' whispered Sam.

With a snort Sam dashed against the man's legs, and again and again he attacked like a small fierce dog, grunting and squealing with anger. The owl swooped down at the man's head and beat him with sharp beak and heavy wings. The mice ran up his trousers and bit his arms and legs. The bit bats fastened their wings in his hair.

'Help! Help! Murder!' cried the man, beating off

the attackers, but his sudden cry aroused Roger in his kennel and Farmer Greensleeves awoke and listened. The hens were cackling, the cock was crowing, the owl was hooting, Sam was squealing and the dog was barking, whilst all the little mice were screeching away.

'Whatever is the matter?' cried the Farmer, hastening to dress, and out he came with his gun. But the man had turned tail and fled down the road.

'What is all this noise, Sam Pig?' asked the Farmer, when he found only little Sam by the broken henhouse door.

'A burglar, Master. I found him. I followed him,' panted Sam, pointing to the sack and wires on the ground.

'Did you rout him all by yourself?' asked the Farmer. 'Did *you* make all that racket?'

'No, Master. I was helped by the owl, the mice and the bit bats,' said Sam, modestly. 'I only did part of it!'

'Owl! Mice! Bit Bats! Where are they?' asked the Farmer, looking round.

'They must have gone back home, Master,' said Sam. 'They live in the cottage down the lane.'

'Primrose Cottage?' asked Mr Greensleeves.

'Yes. The burglar slept there and I slept there and we all slept there,' explained Sam.

'It's a bit puzzling,' said the Farmer. 'Now come in the kitchen, Sam Pig, and have a sup of hot milk and a thank you.'

'No, Master, I'd best go home to Brock the Badger. I've had enough excitement for tonight. I want to go to sleep, Master.'

'Well, take a lantern, Sam,' said the Farmer, lighting a little lantern with glass sides and a pointed top.

'Thank you very much, Sam, for what you've done,' he continued. 'I'll put a double lock on the hen-roost and I'll see to that cottage, too. We mustn't have strangers living in it.'

'No, Master,' said Sam, yawning. 'No, of course not.'

He went away home and he was quite safe, for he carried the little hand-lantern to scare away all bad things.

They were asleep when he arrived, all except Brock the Badger who sat in his armchair waiting.

'Sam, Sam,' said Brock, reproachfully. 'Where have you been?'

'Sleeping in Primrose Cottage,' said Sam, yawning again. 'I ran away and lived there.'

'Did you want to leave us? Are we as bad as all that?' asked Brock, sadly.

'No, Brock. It was only that I want to be alone sometimes,' said Sam.

'We all like to be solitary now and then, Sam. Now go to bed and sleep well. You can tell me about it tomorrow. It's past midnight. Goodnight, Sam.'

'Goodnight, Brock,' murmured Sam. 'I'm glad to be home.'

Sam Pig and the Bouquet

Mollie the dairymaid was going to be married. Mrs Greensleeves was delighted that her kind-hearted maid would live in the thatched cottage down the lane and be able to return each day to look after the dairy work.

Sally the Mare told Sam Pig all about it.

'Our Mollie is getting married,' said Sally one morning, as she and Sam Pig stood by the gate talking.

'Mollie? Our Mollie? Who is she marrying?' asked Sam. 'Nobody is good enough for our Mollie.'

'She is marrying Tony Wildgoose, the thatcher,' said Sally.

'Humph! I like the thatcher quite well,' said Sam, thinking about it. 'Yes. I'll let her marry him. Yes. He thatched the shed in the corner of the field where I shelter when it rains. He leaves little bundles of straw, and I carry them off for straw mattresses. I've got one of his beds at home.'

'Molly likes him too,' agreed Sally. 'They are going to be married and they will live in the thatched cottage with honeysuckle on the porch, down the lane.'

'I know it,' said Sam, eagerly. 'I know it.'

'It's empty. Old Mrs Dobbie has gone to live with her daughter and the cottage is empty. So Mollie and Tony Wildgoose are going to set up house there and Mollie won't leave the farm. She'll come to the dairy as usual. I've heard Mrs Greensleeves telling everybody when we've been out driving.'

'I know that cottage,' said Sam again. 'It isn't empty, Sally. It's full. There isn't room for Mollie. She can't go there at all. It's very full.'

'Full of what?' asked Sally, staring at Sam.

'Full of bats and owls, and cricketing mice, and burglars, and witches and ghostesses,' said Sam.

'My goodness, Sam. Is that true?' asked the startled Mare.

'Yes, Sally. I've met them. That night when the burglar came to rob our hen-roost.'

'I hope Mollie will find out in time,' said Sally. 'I shouldn't like her and Tony Wildgoose to be turned out of their home on their wedding night by all those creatures you've told me about.'

'I think I must talk to her,' said Sam, earnestly.

So without more ado, he went off to the Farm, and tapped at the dairy door.

Mrs Greensleeves came to see who was scratching there.

'Why, Sam Pig,' said she, 'I thought it was a hen. Come in, Sam. Thank you for what you did the other night. Would you like a cheese cake and a drink of butter-milk?'

Sam was surprised at this, but he licked his lips politely, and wiped his feet on the mat, and took off his hat, and kept one hand in his pocket lest the beetles and grasshoppers should escape in Mrs Greensleeves' neat kitchen.

He sipped the butter-milk and ate the cheese cake, in his best manner, refraining from putting the whole cake in his mouth at once.

'I've come for a word with Mollie,' said he, when he had finished. 'Is she about?'

'Yes, Sam. She's in the garden. She'll be back in a minute. Did you know she is going to be married and she will live in that cottage down the lane where you saw the burglar?'

'Yes,' said Sam.

Then Mollie entered, and Sam laughed to see her rosy face, and her smooth cheeks, and smiling eyes.

'Here's a gentleman to see you,' said Mrs Greensleeves, and Sam shyly followed the dairymaid to the dairy.

'Well, Sam. Are you glad I'm getting married?' asked Mollie.

'Yes and no, Mollie. I'm glad of course, but I'm sorry you are thinking of living in Primrose Cottage,' said Sam.

'Why, Sam? It's a lovely little place. It's just right for me and Tony. It's the prettiest little cottage round about. People come to see it, for it's got the old chimney, and beams from Queen Elizabeth's reign. Why don't you want me to live there?'

'Because, Mollie, lots live there already,' said Sam.

'Who lives there? Mrs Dobbie left months ago, and we should have been married earlier if there had been a place to live. Now it's empty.'

'There's lots in it, Mollie. It's full of bats and owls, and mice and burglars and witches and ghostesses,' said Sam, solemnly. 'They'll bite you and nip you and tease you, Mollie.'

'Tony will take care of me, Sam Pig,' said smiling Mollie. 'He'll clear them out. He's going to re-thatch the cottage, for he says there's a regular hive of bats in the old thatch and swarms of mice under the floor boards. He'll make it right for me.'

'I am so glad,' said Sam. Then he added: 'But where will they live, Mollie? They want a home, too. They helped to frighten that burglar away.'

'They'll find somewhere, Sam. There's lots of homes in hollow trees,' said Mollie.

This satisfied Sam, and he was turning away when Mollie called him.

'Sam, I can't very well ask you to my wedding, vicars are so fussy! But you can come to the wedding breakfast afterwards. We shall have a feast here, and Mrs Greensleeves has agreed that I can have a small table set aside for you and your family. I will send an invitation.'

'Oh, Mollie! Oh, Mollie!' gasped Sam. 'What an

honour! Oh! I don't think Brock the Badger will come, but we four pigs will come with pleasure.'

'Then goodbye, Sam. I have a lot of work to do. Thank you for warning me about the cottage.'

'Goodbye, Mollie,' said Sam. He walked out, and then he ran very fast to spread the good news.

First he told the Mare about it, and Sally was delighted.

'Are you going, Sally?' asked Sam.

'Yes, I have to take the guests to the wedding,' said Sally. 'I've been to weddings before. I shall be decorated, with ribbons on the harness and a white bow on the whip and flowers in the lamps instead of candles, and white flowers on my head-band. Mollie will wear a white dress, and she'll ride in the cart, for Mrs Greensleeves will look after her. She has no mother, and Mrs Greensleeves will be kind to her.'

'A white dress, same as Ann's Sunday frock!' said Sam. 'What shall I wear, Sally? Shall I carry flowers?'

'If you like, Sam,' said Sally. 'Mollie will have a bouquet!'

'Tell me about the feast,' said Sam.

'There's to be a big white cake covered with icing, and Mollie will cut it and give you a bit, and she'll bring a scrap for me out in the yard,' said Sally.

'Don't tell me any more,' cried Sam. 'It is too much for me. Never in all my days, never, even when the Mermaid came to see us and Lady Echo and the little

Princess, never have I heard so much good news. I am quite full.'

Sam took to his heels, as if he thought the happiness would be spilled if he stayed any longer, and he went home to tell Brock the Badger and Ann, Tom and Bill Pig.

Brock smoked his pipe and listened. 'You are right, Sam. I shall not go to the wedding, but you must all go. You must be clean and tidy. You must all have baths and a good scrub.'

'Oh dear,' sighed Sam.

'You must have your clothes washed and patched,' continued Brock. 'We shall want to give Mollie a present. I'll look through my own treasures buried in the cave in the wood. There may be something I've dug up from past ages.'

'Not a bone,' said Sam. 'Mollie won't like a bone.'

'Certainly not,' said Brock, indignantly. 'Do you think I am an ignorant pig like yourself! I was thinking of a treasure of past days, a bronze tankard, or a crock of gold or a bracelet of early times, buried deep and forgotten for a thousand years.'

Sam apologized humbly, and the others cuffed him for his stupidity.

'Mollie will carry a bouquet,' said he, changing the subject. 'We might make her a bouquet of our own. Ann knows about flowers, and she won the prize at the Flower Show.'

'A good idea, Sam,' said Brock. 'You must find some nice flowers and make a pretty bunch. Now be off and wash your clothes and yourselves, and tidy your things and mend and patch.'

The next days were full of washing and sewing and patching. Sam's trousers were very dirty, and Ann said he must have them scrubbed and mended with new patches of bright stuff, dyed scarlet and yellow and green with herbal dyes.

What a gathering of sheep's wool from the hedges there was, and a dyeing and a collecting of odds and ends from the Farmhouse scrap bag! Ann sewed the pieces together and made some new clothing of many colours, with flowers for ornament, and stitchery of grasses.

The invitation to the wedding came and Brock framed the piece of paste-board in straw and fastened it to the wall of the house for all to look at the silver letters. Only Sam could read it, and he had to miss out the long words, but it didn't matter, for they all knew what it was about.

'We must gather the flowers for the bouquet,' said Sam. 'It's no use getting buttercups and daisies, which Mollie sees every day. We must get something special, like bee orchis and butterfly orchis, spider orchis and frog orchis, fly orchis and greenman orchis, and lady's slipper.'

The others stared at him.

'Oh, Sam! We don't know where to find all those

rare flowers. Let's give bees and butterflies and frogs and spiders, in a basket, all looking pretty.'

'No. Mollie wouldn't like that. I'll go out and find them in the woods and on the hills,' said Sam.

'I'm going to give a bouquet of vegetables,' said Bill. 'That will be more useful than those rare flowers. I'll get onions and carrots and leeks and a cabbage for Mollie.'

'I'll make her a little wedding cake,' said Tom. Tom cooked a wonderful cake, which contained a bit of everything in the store cupboard, mixed with a honeycomb and a lot of eggs. It was baked and then iced with sugar, and Tom put a bunch of roses made from the snowy pith of rushes on the top. The white petals were strips of curved delicate pith, from under the green rind of the rushes in the field.

Bill wanted to thatch the cake with straw, but Sam was sure Mollie would prefer the icing.

Brock the Badger turned over his treasures which he kept in a secret underground cave. He looked at rings and necklaces, and bowls and plates of bronze and gold and silver, black with age. Finally he chose a little bronze tankard with fine ornament on the sides and two little handles. He cleaned it and polished it and made it shine like new.

Poor Sam wandered over the fields and woods, seeking rare flowers. He picked a bunch of orchis, but they were not striking enough for a wedding bouquet. Ann said she would give them to Mollie, as her own bunch, and Sam could find something better.

On the morning of the wedding day Sam passed the lodge gates of the Big House. He saw a fiery patch of colour in a flower bed near the drive.

'Those red flowers would do,' said Sam, eyeing them with pleasure. 'They would show up. Mollie would see them a long way off. I'll get a bunch.'

So through the gates he went and nobody stopped him. The lodge keeper saw Sam's little check trousers swishing round the corner and he took no further notice.

'There's that Sam Pig, gone to see the Irish cook again,' he told his wife. 'I expect she gives him scraps.' Then he went back to his newspaper.

But Sam never saw the Irish cook. Instead he visited the geranium bed, and he picked every flower in it. Then, with his nose buried in the rich warm-scented flowers, he returned home.

'It's the best bouquet ever known,' Sam boasted. 'Mollie will like it, and Ann will think I am a clever pigling and all will be well.'

He wasn't quite sure about Brock, so he hid the bunch under a bucket until they started.

'I've got my bouquet ready,' he announced.

'And I've got a present for you to take,' said Brock.

'I've got the little bunch of bee orchis,' said Ann, holding out the tiny nosegay of lovely flowers, tied with grasses.

'And I've got a vegetable bouquet,' said Bill, showing his carrots and onions, mixed with herbs and grasses.

'And here is the cake,' said Tom, holding up his small cake, with the roses on the top.

Brock went off to the woods and the four little pigs went to the wedding. They stood by the farm gate and looked through the bars at the farmyard, where Sally the Mare was already in the cart shafts. She had flowers on her head, bells on her harness, white ribbons on the whip and among the reins. Flowers filled the glass lamps, and everything was so beautiful the little pigs were speechless with admiration.

Then Mollie came out in her white dress, with a veil on her head instead of a sun-bonnet, orange blossom in her straight gold hair, and some roses in her hands.

'Hurrah! Hurrah!' called the little pigs as the trap drove off with Farmer Greensleeves and Mollie, Mrs Greensleeves and the children.

'Now we must wait till they come back,' said Sam. 'We'll go to the barn and sit there in the hay so that we keep clean.'

They rested on the bales of hay, and they listened to the clucking of hens, the mooing of cows, the crowing of the cock. Everything seemed to say that Mollie was getting married that day. The church bells were ringing far away in the valley, and the river was tossing and foaming, so that they could hear the sound of it mingled with the bells. It was so sweet in the hay that they all fell asleep.

The wedding was over, and the little pigs were wakened by the carts and traps bringing guests to the farm. They waited to be invited indoors. At last when the guests were all settled at the great oak table in the farm kitchen, someone remembered the four little pigs. Dick Greensleeves went out to find them.

They followed Dick rather shyly. Sam carried the big bouquet of geraniums with the wedding present, Tom carried the cake, Ann held her bee orchis, and Bill had the vegetable bunch.

They sat down at their own small table, and the people turned round and stared at them, and laughed and joked at Mollie's friends. The little pigs behaved nicely and kept very quiet. They ate and drank politely from their bowls and dishes, and they tasted the small pieces of wedding cake. It was all very strange and very nice, but rather uncomfortable to sit so long without rolling on the floor or making a loud squeak.

Sam clutched the geraniums, as he waited for a chance to give them to Mollie, and the present was somewhere, Sam wasn't quite sure where he had put it.

Suddenly all eyes were turned to the little table where the animals sat. Farmer Greensleeves stood up and called to Sam.

'You must make a speech, Sam,' said Farmer

Greensleeves, and they all rapped on the table and cried: 'Speech, speech.'

Sam blushed, and stood up, nervously holding the great bouquet of geraniums, so that his face was nearly hidden.

'Give it to me,' whispered Ann Pig, and she slipped it on his empty chair, out of the way.

'Ladies and gentlemen,' began Sam. 'I wish good health and happiness to Mollie the dairymaid.'

'Here, here,' clapped the people.

'Everywhere,' said Sam. 'And I hope she will live in her cottage with my friend the thatcher, and no bats, nor owls, nor mice, nor burglars, nor witches, nor ghostesses for company. Now I have great pleasure in presenting Mollie with a present from the four Pigs and Brock the Badger. Brock dug it up in the Nightingale Wood, when he was making a good hole in the ground. Here it is.'

There were loud cheers as Sam paused and felt in his pocket, and then in his hat. He dived under the table and hunted about, and all the little pigs joined him with grunts and squeals. 'Where is it? Have you lost it? Where can it be?'

Then Ann gave a cry and brought something out of a bundle of hay that had been lying by their feet. It was the bronze tankard, with little ornaments on the sides.

Sam held up the beautiful thing, for all to admire.

'How lovely!' cried Mollie. 'Oh, Sam!'

'Brock the Badger says that it belonged to the ancient Britons, and as he is an ancient Briton, he hopes you will like it, Mollie. Brock says he has put some of his magic in it, Mollie. Brock says that if you put water in it, then it will taste like wine, and when you drink it you will forget your troubles.' Sam held out the shining old tankard and Mollie, in her bridal dress, came forward to take it.

Everyone clapped, and Sam clapped too. Then he sat down with a thump, thankful that the speech was over. There was a crushing sound, as he sat on something very soft.

'Oh!' cried little Ann Pig. 'You've sat on the bouquet, Sam.'

Like a Jack-in-the-box he sprang to his feet again, and took the bunch of geraniums.

There was great laughter as he held them ruefully out to Mollie.

'This is my present of a bouquet, Mollie,' said he, sadly. 'I've sat on them. They are quite flat, Mollie. Quite flat.'

'Never mind, Sam. They smell as sweet,' said Mollie, pressing her burning face in the scented flowers.

'And they haven't lost their colour, Sam,' added Farmer Greensleeves.

'I shall dry the petals and make a cushion of them,' said Mollie quickly. 'Thank you very much, Sam Pig, Bill Pig, Ann Pig, Tom Pig, and Brock the Badger. Thank you, my dear friends.'

Then Tom, Bill and Ann gave their own little presents to Mollie.

They drank the health of Mollie and her Tony the thatcher, and the little pigs sipped cowslip wine, which made them cough and splutter.

Then Mollie went off in her pretty white dress with her rose bouquet and her geranium bouquet in her hands, and her husband carried the magical tankard. They walked down the lane to their cottage and everyone threw confetti after them, but the little pigs threw dandelion clocks.

'A lovely wedding,' said Mrs Greensleeves. 'And those four pigs added to the fun. They were well-behaved, too, and they didn't gobble their food.'

'I said they were good pigs,' said Farmer Greensleeves. 'It was just like Sam to sit on the bouquet.'

The little pigs were running home to tell Brock the Badger all about the wedding. They carried a bag of scraps and a piece of wedding cake.

'It was wonderful,' cried Sam. 'She liked the present very much, Brock. I sat on my bouquet, but Mollie didn't mind. It was just as pretty.'

'I never saw your bouquet, Sam. You kept it dark. What kind of flowers did you get?' asked Brock.

'Geraniums,' said Sam.

'Where from, Sam?' asked Brock.

'I took 'em from the Big House,' said Sam.

But up at the Big House they were all asking how the geraniums that filled the large front bed had disappeared when no one had been seen except a little pig.

The Singing Gate

Sam Pig went out to swing on the big gate one fine morning. This was no ordinary gate to a garden or field path, or even to a ploughfield with a scarecrow in the middle. It was a five-barred gate of oak, which shut in Farmer Greensleeves' best field of meadow grass for haymaking. It was the gate where Sally the Mare often lingered to gaze at the hills and the sky and the tree-tops. It was the gate that shut with such a resounding clang that the echo of it rang through the countryside, to tell all people that Farmer Greensleeves' best meadow was not to be entered until the grass had grown long, and the haymakers and mowers had arrived for the hay-harvest.

Sam liked this gate for many reasons. It was his own meeting place with Sally the Mare. He could count on her being there most evenings when she wasn't in the stable. It was the gate Sam climbed when he wanted to mount on Sally's back. Best of all, it was a singing gate.

Sam swung backwards and forwards on it, when it wasn't shut to keep the mowing grass safe, and the gate sang with a shrill cry, going up and down the scale with the motion. Sam loved this gate-music. He, too, sang when the gate sang and together they made a loud squealing noise like a dozen pigs squeezed in a farm cart together.

> *'Sam Pig, Sam Pig, every afternoon,*
> *Come and sit along o' me, and sing a little tune,'*

went the gate, in its cheerful inviting voice.

Little Sam Pig listened to it, with his head aside and his ears cocked. Then he replied in his own sing-song :

> *'Oak gate, meadow gate,*
> *I'll sit along o' you.*
> *I'm weary of my family,*
> *I wants to be with you.'*

Then, after some more swinging and singing, the gate would shut itself fast to the gate-post, and Sam knew that the song was finished. It was time for something else to happen.

'Let's have a tale now,' Sam would say, and the gate rumbled and mumbled, and shook its wooden gate-post, and rattled its iron latch as it thought deep in its oaken heart. Then, with little soft murmurs like the droppings of shavings from a carpenter's plane, the gate began to talk.

'Once upon a time I was a young oak tree in yonder wood,' it began, and Sam's blue eyes opened wide. Over the field was a wood where the pheasants lived, and the trees grew close together making a deep black shade. It was a wood on a hillside, with rocks sticking out like dragons, and, indeed, one of these rocks was a real dragon, which had fallen asleep a thousand years ago. It was a wood with many wild flowers in the glades, and a game-keeper's tree, where robber birds hung. Sam never ventured in this wood, for he was afraid of the game-keeper. He always ran on the tiny footpath which skirted the trees, but occasionally he poked his nose over the wall, or he hunted for bilberries on the bushes at the wood's edge. In this enchanted wood, with its dragon, its giants, and fairies, the oak tree had been born.

'When I was a young oak tree, I sheltered a man running away from those who were after him. He climbed my boughs, and I spread my leaves over his face to hide him,' said the gate.

'Who was after him?' asked Sam. 'A bear?'

'No, some men dressed in armour: soldiers they were. He was a King Charles man, so I heard afterwards. I hid him and kept him safe, and a friend at the farm brought him food and looked after him, until he could escape.'

'Did he say Thank you?' asked Sam.

'Yes, Sam, he did. Years afterwards he returned and found me and cut a little cross of thankfulness on my trunk.'

'I should like to save somebody,' said Sam, slowly stroking the gate.

'You never know,' said the gate. 'Now you tell me a tale, Sam. It's your turn.'

Sam began the tale of the circus, with its wonders, and he was in the middle of it, with the oak gate listening with all its ears, when Sally came up.

'Farmer Greensleeves is bringing the young bull to this meadow,' said Sally. 'You'd best get out of the way, Sam.'

'Why?' asked Sam. 'I likes bulls. They roar and stamp.'

'You won't like this one,' said Sally, sharply. 'So move away. He's a fierce fellow, bad-tempered too. He won't be here very long, it's my opinion.'

The Farmer and his man came across the field with a young bull with a ring in his nose, and a pole holding him from them. Sam scuttled away and watched from the shelter of the hedge. Sally strolled off and began to eat the grass. The man opened the gate and the bull was turned into the field.

'I'll lock this gate, for it's a danger place,' said Farmer Greensleeves. 'Nobody must come in with that young demon. They won't want to stop very long if they do get in.'

The bull galloped off with his tail uplifted like a question mark. Farmer Greensleeves took a padlock from his pocket and locked the gate. Then he caught sight of Sam squinting from the hedge.

'No more swinging on the gate for a while, Sam,'

said he. 'Not while the bull is here. Gate's got to be kept shut.'

Sam nodded. 'No, Master. I'll sit on the gate but I won't unfasten it,' said he. 'I can listen to the tales just the same.'

The Farmer put up a notice, 'Beware of the Bull' and went away. Sam and Sally came close to look at it.

'What does it say?' asked Sally. 'You can read it, can't you, Sam?'

Sam slowly spelled the words.

'Bee and Bull,' said he. 'B is for Brock the Badger. Something to do with Brock and Bees and Bull,' he informed Sally.

' 'Ware Bull,' said the gate. 'I've had this before.'

Sam climbed up and sat on the top bar to get a good look at the young bull.

'What's the matter, Bull?' called Sam, as the bull rushed up and down, but the beast only roared angrily. Then it began to eat the good sweet grass and Sam forgot all about it.

'This gate and me is telling tales,' said Sam to Sally. 'We are good friends, we are.'

'This gate is a special one,' agreed Sally. 'The children at the farm call it the Wishing Gate. They come here and make their wishes.'

'Do the wishes come true?' asked Sam.

'I can't tell you for certain. It depends what you mean by true. I only know what I've heard. Often and often, young Dick has ridden on my back to this gate

and here he has stopped and put a hand on the top bar
where you're sitting and made a wish.'

'What did he wish for?' asked Sam. 'Surely he has
everything in the world – a farm and you, and lots to
eat!'

'He wished not to have to go to school, and not to
have to go to bed, and then he wanted to see the circus, and he asked for a football,' said Sally.

'What then?' demanded Sam.

'Well, he fell off the haystack and hurt his leg, so he
didn't have to go to school. He got that wish. He
stayed up late and he was so tired he begged to go to
bed, so he got that wish. He went to the circus, and
he had a football, so his wishes came true,' said Sally.

'Can I make a wish?' asked Sam.

'Of course you can, Sam. You've made many a wish,
on stars and moons, and now make one at our old
Wishing Gate.'

'I wish . . . I wish . . .' began Sam, and then there
was a shout. A man was running in the field and the
bull was after him.

'He shouldn't have come,' said Sam. 'He was picking our mushrooms. He must have climbed the far
wall. If he'd come this way he would have seen the
notice.'

Sally watched the man with anxiety. The bull was
getting nearer, and the man ran this way and that in
terror. The heavy strong animal kept its head lowered, and its sharp wicked horns were ready to toss

the man. He tried to climb the wall, but there was no foothold and he ran desperately towards the gate across the wide field.

'Poor fellow,' said Sally. 'He can't run fast enough. He's too fat. He'll be caught.'

Sam made up his mind. He put his short little legs over the top bar and slid to the ground. Then he ran towards the bull, shouting and waving his hat. The bull's attention was diverted for a moment.

'What's this?' he roared, turning his great head to Sam, and his blood-shot eyes glared. 'Who's this impudent creature?'

He made a rush at Sam, and the man sprinted to the gate and got over in a flash. There stood Sally the Mare with her nose raised, as she whinnied to encourage Sam.

'Run! Sam, run!' she called, in her own language, and the man stared at Sally and then watched the race in the field. Sam dodged one way and the bull dodged the same. Then Sam made a dive under the bull's nose and came out behind his legs. That gave him a chance, and as the bull looked down to find him, Sam flew with all four legs twinkling, and little tail outstretched and little mouth calling: 'Wee, wee, wee,' just like an ordinary little pig in a farmyard.

'Come on, Sam,' called Sally, and the man at the gate clapped his hands and shouted, 'Run, little 'un. Run.'

Sam scuttled to the gate and scrambled over just in

time, for the bull arrived as Sam dropped safely to the other side.

'Well run, Sam,' said Sally, licking him with her soft tongue.

'It's a pig,' muttered the man. 'One of Farmer Greensleeves' pets. Well, he's saved my bacon!'

Then he looked up and saw the notice, 'Beware of the Bull'.

'A bit late,' said he, 'but better late than never.'

Sam looked at him and he looked at Sam. 'They'll not believe it when I tell 'em at the "Pig and Whistle" tonight,' said he. 'But it's true, isn't it, young pig? You did save me, didn't you?'

Sam nodded, with never a word. Then the little pig picked up a dandelion and stuck it in his mouth.

'It's true. I'm not dreaming,' said the man, walking away. 'There's the bull and there's the pig and here am I, Samuel Ramsbottom. But they won't believe it, down at the "Pig and Whistle".'

'He never said "Thank you",' murmured Sam, sadly. He climbed on the gate and watched the bull. In the distance lay a red spotted handkerchief full of mushrooms the man had dropped in his flight.

'I think I'll get those for Tom to cook for supper,' said Sam.

'Best wait a bit,' advised Sally. 'Wait till the bull lies down and takes a nap. He won't be long. He's upset and cross. Don't bother him now.'

So Sam sat on the gate waiting, and as he sat he sang another song to the old gate:

'*Sam Pig, Ann Pig, Tom, Bill and Brock,*
Went swinging on the old gate to taste the lock.
The gate was made of oakenwood, the lock was made
   of money,
The latch was sugar candy and the gate-posts sweetest
   honey.'

'That's a queer 'un,' said Sally, as she listened to Sam.

'It's my imagination,' said Sam, airily. 'You never know what might happen.'

'No, you're right about that,' agreed Sally.

'I'm hungry after that run,' said Sam. 'I could eat some sugar candy and honey now this minute.'

He leaned close to the latch and put out his little pink tongue. He took a lick and another lick. It was sweet as sugar candy. Then he licked the gate-post. It was sweet as honey. A bee rose from it, and left a morsel there it had just taken from the cloverpatch.

'Sally. Sally. My wish has come true,' cried Sam, and he licked again.

Sally stared at Sam and then she too came to the gate. She rubbed her nose on it. Indeed the latch was sweet-tasting.

'You've done it, Sam. I feel sugar on my lips, and there's a taste of honey round the gate-posts.'

They both were silent while they licked and suddenly Sam laughed.

'There's nothing. It was my imagination, Sally.'

'A powerful imagination to make sugar candy and honey out of an old gate,' said Sally. 'But there's the bull gone to sleep, and you've got a chance.'

Sam ran off, dancing softly, past the snoring bull to the far part of the field and he returned with the red handkerchief full of mushrooms.

'I wanted a new hanky,' said he. 'This is my reward.' He ate a few fresh button mushrooms and then strolled away with Sally. They both walked to the barn and there they nibbled brown linseed cake, put ready for the cows.

'I like cow-cake,' said Sam Pig.

It was good solid food and they felt better for it. Sam filled his pocket with the cake, and then he made a little whistle pipe from an oaten straw.

'You go home now,' said Sally. 'I've to do some work for Master, and you go home.'

Sam said goodnight, but he went round by the singing gate for a last word and a look at the bull. The fierce animal was quietly grazing and when Sam played a tune on his whistle pipe, it came to the gate.

'Sorry I was so fierce today, Sam,' it said, apologetically. 'That man roused me, and I was hot and tired and thirsty. I feel better now.'

'It's all right,' said Sam, amiably offering the cow-cake to the bull. I quite understand. I feel that way myself often when Tom has been teasing me.'

The bull settled down on one side of the gate, and

Sam stretched out his hand and stroked the bull's nose. A little song came out of the air, and perhaps it was the gate singing, for it cannot have been the bull. This is what Sam heard:

> *'Over the hills to China*
> *Over the mountains to Spain.*
> *Carry him off to dreamland,*
> *And bring him back again.'*

The gate gently rocked Sam, till he fell asleep. He rolled down and lay curled up by the bull. There Farmer Greenseeves found him when he went at dusk to look at his animal.

'Sam Pig. What are you doing here?' he cried, and he lifted Sam up by his trousers and set him at the right side of the gate.

Sam rubbed his eyes and yawned. Then he picked up his whistle pipe and looked at the sleeping bull.

'Oh, Master. I've been taming the bull,' said he. 'Then the gate sang a song to me and I fell asleep.'

'I'm not surprised at anything you do or anything the old gate does,' said the Farmer. 'Now you go home quick before anything catches you. Where did you get that red handkerchief?'

'It was a mushroomer's hanky, and the bull made him run,' said Sam, and both he and the Farmer laughed.

The Farmer put a hand in one of his big pockets and brought out a rosy apple. He put his hand in another pocket and brought out a juicy pear. He felt in his left hand trouser pocket and found a few hum-bugs. He felt in his right-hand pocket and found a piece of sugar-candy.

'Here, take these, Sam. They'll do for your supper,' said he. 'I always keep a few bits in my pockets to eat when I'm peckish.'

'Oh, thank you, Master,' said Sam, joyfully. 'I wish I had all those pockets. I would fill them with food for a week.'

He ran off, hurrying home to Brock the Badger, who was standing by the door looking up at the moon, and counting the early stars.

'Brock,' he cried. 'I've been to sleep. I needn't go to bed. I've had a dream, Brock.'

'What did you dream?' asked Brock.

'I dreamt I went to China and to Spain,' said Sam.

'What were they like, Sam?' asked little Ann, running up when she heard her young brother's voice.

'China was full of dragons, and Spain was full of cats,' said Sam. 'I was just inviting them to come home with me when Farmer Greensleeves woke me up.'

'Come indoors and sit by the fire,' invited Brock. 'I'll tell you a tale about a badger who went to China and brought a blue dragon home with him.'

So they sat with Brock and listened to his story, while the clock ticked, and the fire crackled, and the kettle sang on the hearth.

'I'm glad we live here,' said Ann, cosily. 'I like a little house all by itself, and nobody can find it, because Brock has magicked it. Then no dragons and cats can come.'

'I saved a man today,' said Sam, suddenly. 'I saved him and he gave me his handkerchief for a reward. At least, I took it.'

'Did you save him from a dragon?' asked Tom Pig.

'No, from a raging bull,' replied Sam, casually. 'I was a bull-fighter.'

'Then you really went to Spain, Sam,' said Brock. 'That's where the bull-fighters live.'

'I suppose I did,' said Sam. 'Yes, I fought the bull and then I fed him on cow-cake. Yes. That's all.'

Sam Pig and the Wheelbarrow

'There's just one thing I want more nor anything,' said Sam Pig one morning, softly, as if he were talking to himself. Bill and Tom bustled about, wiping dishes, chasing wasps and spiders from the house. Ann was dusting the chairs and clock. Brock the Badger sat by the open door, looking at his pocket book, turning the greeny-brown faded pages.

'There's just one thing I want,' murmured Sam, staring at the ceiling as if the thing were up there. Then he went to the window and looked out at the wild garden, the woods and hills.

'More nor anything,' he added sadly.

'What do you want?' asked Ann.

'Just one thing? Why, he always wants *something*,' cried Bill, impatiently. 'There are twenty things young Sam wants.'

'What is it?' asked Ann.

'It's a wheelbarrow,' said Sam. 'A barrow with wheels.'

'What do you want a wheelbarrow for?' asked Bill.

'To wheel things in, of course,' murmured Sam, in a doleful voice.

'What kind of things?' asked Tom.

'Anything. Anything I find. Just anything,' said Sam. 'I can't carry much, but if I had a wheelbarrow I could wheel them home.'

'Did you hear what I said, Sam? What kind of things?' asked Bill.

'Dragons and witches and unicorns,' sneered Tom, and he flicked the dishcloth at Sam's head.

'No, Tom. I would get mushrooms and herbs and heather for our beds, and maybe a sheaf of corn,' returned Sam, dodging the cloth.

'There's a wheelbarrow in the garden,' said Tom. 'Why can't you use that?'

'I want a little one, all my own.' Sam ruffled his ears and nodded his small pink head. 'All my very own. A wheelbarrow nobody else can take and I'd wheel it and wheel it every day.'

Brock the Badger wrote a word in his notebook and then he looked at Sam. He seemed to awake from a dream.

'Come along out,' said he, yawning, then rising and stretching himself. 'Did I hear wheelbarrow? Why are you all talking about wheelbarrows this morning? Are you going to do some gardening?'

'It's young Sam,' explained Bill. 'He wants a wheelbarrow all his own to carry things about.'

'Very good idea,' said Brock, but Tom sprang at Sam, seized his hind legs and lifted them, so that Sam had to throw himself on his front legs.

'I'll show you a wheelbarrow,' laughed Tom, and he wheeled the little pig on his two front legs, like a pink wheelbarrow, until Sam struggled and escaped.

They all followed Brock the Badger out to the fields, walking under the hedges in single file, where nobody would see them, and soon their quarrels were forgotten in the scents of the earth, and the many sights of strange happenings that always occur in the depths of the country.

Tom gathered firewood from the fallen twigs of the trees, and Bill looked for birds' nests. Ann found flowers – bluebells, red campion, and a delicate flower called fumitory, which Brock said was the smoke-flower rising from invisible chimneys underground.

Sam ran backward and forward, hiding in the holly bushes, where he found many a secret home, climbing the low trees which had a foothold near the earth, swinging from the dipping branches of the beeches, which held out their long boughs ready for anyone who liked to play.

Brock cut a slip of newly-grown ash and whittled a musical pipe from it. Then he played a tune which lured the birds from the trees and brought them down to look at him.

A turtle dove, and a chattering jay, a spry black-bird and a cuckoo came to the call of the Badger.

'Hello, Brock the Badger,' said they. 'Hello, Sam Pig. How are you today?'

'Very well, thank you,' said Sam.

'You called us, Brock,' said the turtle dove.

'We all came,' said the jay, the cuckoo and the blackbird.

'Keep an eye on young Sam,' said Brock. 'Don't let him fly too high. Keep his wings clipped.'

'We will,' said the birds, and they laughed together with little short cries; they hopped up and down and ate a few crumbs Brock took from his pocket. Then they fluttered and rose and flew away, singing their songs.

'I say, Brock,' said Sam, indignantly. 'I don't want those chattering birds. The dove always saying "Tak two coos, taffy. Tak two," and the cuckoo calling "Cuckoo, cuckoo," and the jay screeching murder, and the blackbird whistling like mad. I'm not a baby.'

They all laughed at Sam, and then they played hide and seek, which is an exciting game in the tall green bracken.

Tom had made a heap of sticks and they divided them to carry under their arms.

'If I had a wheelbarrow, I could take all these and more home for our fire,' said Sam, suddenly remembering the wheelbarrow.

They stopped by the river and watched the little fish swimming around, but no mermaid sunned herself on the rock in the water, no bright hair gleamed in the waves.

'If I had a wheelbarrow I could pop the fish and the river into it and wheel it home,' said Sam.

They came to a bluebell wood, blue as a piece of the sky.

'If I had a wheelbarrow . . .' began Sam, but Tom leapt at him in indignation.

'If *I* had a wheelbarrow,' said Brock, suddenly, 'I should put young Sam in it and wheel him over the edge of the world and drop him out to the stars.' This alarmed Sam and he said no more.

When Sam was in bed that night, warm under his blanket, and Bill, Tom and Ann were fast asleep in their rooms, Brock opened the door and looked out.

There was a new moon in the sky, a little slip of gold in the blue. Brock had already bowed to the Mistress of Heaven, and now he looked up for a few minutes and made a wish. Then he closed the door and padded away, through the fields and woods to a clearing where the woodsmen had been felling trees.

He found a few suitable pieces of oak and he set to work to make a wheelbarrow. He took a small adze from his pocket and shaved the wood. From his back pocket he drew a queer stumpy saw, and with a stone for a hammer and a few pegs he made the body of the wheelbarrow. He took a slice of a small tree the woodsman had thrown down and he shaped it for the heavy little wheel. Then he slung it on his back and padded home again, stepping softly through the grasses, never breaking a twig as he walked.

In the kitchen he examined his work. The two

handles and the two short legs were firm, and the wheel spun round on the axle when he touched it. Finally he reached up to the shelf where he kept his ointments, his medicines and his magic potions. He pushed these aside and hunted for a pot of paint.

It was a strange old pot, with many colours in it, for every time Brock dipped his brush in the paint, a a different colour came out. The wheelbarrow was striped like a rainbow when Brock had finished.

He left it to dry, and then he wiped the brush, and returned the paint pot to the back of the shelf.

Once more he opened the door, and now the moon had gone. Then Brock, too, went out to hunt, to meet his badger friends, to walk the lonely woods and moors in the darkness of the night.

The next morning Sam Pig rolled out of bed and came running downstairs, to wash himself in the brook near the back door, where he always filled the kettle. He liked to be there before the others so that he could splash and play in the water.

So he raced down to the little room and there on the hearth was the sparkling wheelbarrow, shot-silk, green and gold, blue and lavender, and Sam knew at once that Brock had made it.

'Oh, dear old Brock!' cried Sam. 'Dear good Brock! He knew my heart's desire. A wheelbarrow to carry things in.'

He trundled it out of doors, while he washed himself, and then he trundled it down the lane. He found

mushrooms and roots, flowers and leaves, a snail in her shell and a poor wounded bird.

Then he rumbled back with the little wheel bumping over the rough patches of earth, and the wheelbarrow swaying to and fro as he wheeled it.

The others had come down, and they were already getting the breakfast. Tom opened his mouth to scold Sam, but when he saw the wheelbarrow he could say nothing but, 'Oh. Oh.'

'My goodness, Sam! You are a lucky pig,' said Bill. 'It's the neatest little barrow I've ever seen.'

'What have you got in it, Sam dear?' asked Ann.

They looked at the leaves, the flowers, the snail in her shell and the wounded bird, the mushrooms and the roots.

The mushrooms and the roots they cooked for breakfast, and the flowers and leaves they put in a jug to deck the table. The snail came out of her shell and sat on the table-cloth, with a little bowl and a spoon of mother-of-pearl in her lap, ready to join with the family. The little bird fluttered her feathers and opened her eyes, and then she flew to a chair and began to sing a song.

'I'm well again. I was hurt, I was dying, and now I am well. Thank you, all you who have cured me,' said she, and away through the open door she went.

'I didn't make her well,' said Sam. 'I picked her up and brought her home to bury her. I thought she was nearly dead.'

Then Brock came in, with a bag of food on his back. His feet and legs were wet, he was dirty and tired, but happy with the night's tramp for many a mile.

'Oh, Brock! Thank you! Brock, thank you!' cried Sam.

'I met a bird down the lane, singing with all its might,' said Brock. 'Do you know anything about it?'

'It flew out of the house,' explained Sam. 'I brought it home, wounded by somebody, in my wheelbarrow, and it got well and flew away.'

'Ah,' cried Brock. 'I just wondered.'

They had breakfast, talking very fast, and the snail ate her grain of porridge and sang in a soft, slippery whisper.

> *'I have a little cupboard,*
> *Deep in my shell.*
> *There I keep my jewels,*
> *Like water in a well.'*

She fished in her house and opened the cupboard door and took out a tiny jewel made of a drop of dew and gave it to Ann.

'Please put me on a grass blade,' she whispered, and Ann carried her with her striped house to the tall grasses in the wild garden.

But Brock and Sam and Tom and Bill were eating and talking so hard they never noticed.

Sam took his wheelbarrow across the fields to show to Sally the Mare.

'What have you got there?' asked Sally, when Sam came trundling the little wheelbarrow over the grass. 'Is it a bunch of hothouse flowers? Is it a peacock's feathers? Is it a piece of a rainbow?'

'It's a wheelbarrow,' said Sam, proudly. 'Brock made it for me. He painted it for me and he put just a touch of magic, Sally. Don't tell anyone. Keep it secret. There's just a little drop of magic in it. Not much.'

'What can it do?' asked Sally.

'Well, I found a wounded bird, and brought it home in the wheelbarrow and it was cured, Sally.'

'Then you can do lots of things, Sam,' said Sally, and she tossed a bunch of hay into the wheelbarrow. The shrivelled grasses uncurled, their brown turned to green and they lay, fresh as if just gathered.

Sam invited a poorly hen to rest in the wheelbarrow, and when she shook her head, and squatted close to the ground in misery, Sally spoke to her, too.

'Come along, my dear,' said Sally. 'Sam won't hurt you. He has a magical wheelbarrow that will put new life in you.'

So the hen struggled to her feet, and Sam helped her into the wheelbarrow, where she lay, limp and bedraggled with lack-lustre eyes.

'I feel very sick,' she murmured, and she fell asleep. So Sam wheeled her up and down and Sally stood near, waiting for something to happen.

In a few minutes, her eyes opened, her feathers

were bright, and she stood up, clucking and thanking Sam. Then down she flew, and away to the farm she hurried to get some corn before the others had eaten it.

'Well, Sam,' said Sally. 'You've got something there. You can't cure my headache and my backache, for I can never sit in your wheelbarrow, but you can help all small creatures, birds and butterflies and little animals in the woods.'

'It all depends,' said Sam, solemnly. 'It depends how long the magic lasts.'

A few days later the wheelbarrow did nothing at all. It carried wood for the fires, and plants for the garden, and roots for the cooking pot, and flowers for sister Ann, but a little bird whose wing was broken was the same after its journey and Brock had to set the wing. The colours of the wheelbarrow faded, too, and lost their beauty.

But when the new moon shone in the sky, the magical powers returned.

'It all depends on the new moon,' explained Brock. 'I made it at the new moon, and some magic must have crept into it, without my knowing. So as the moon waxes the power grows, but when the moon changes, the magic fades. A good thing, too, Sam. We can't have you doing strange things, for you are only an ordinary little pigling, you know.'

'I didn't ask for a magical wheelbarrow,' protested Sam. 'I just wanted an ordinary wheelbarrow to wheel things in. But I'm glad it's a magical wheelbarrow, Brock.'

At the next new moon the wheelbarrow became strong and able to heal the small creatures of the woodland when Sam wheeled them about. In between times Sam filled the wheelbarrow with potatoes and carried them for the farmer, and they remained potatoes and didn't change to plums and peaches as they did at the new moon. He took turnips to the sheep, from the turnip field, and he gleaned corn from the harvest fields for the hens in the farmyard.

He carried firewood for Brock's fire, and sandstone to clean the stone floor, and rushes to throw down as rugs. He became such a useful little pig that Tom tweaked his ears and said he thought Sam was growing wings.

Then Sam went to collect frogs and worms and snakes and creepy-crawlies. He brought them home in his wheelbarrow, singing as he went —

> *'Through lanes broad and narrow,*
> *I wheel my wheelbarrow,*
> *With creepies and crawlies and snakes alive-O.'*

When Tom opened the door Sam emptied them all out on the floor.

'I've brought a few friends to visit you,' said he, and away he darted with his wheelbarrow before Tom could catch him again.

Christmas at Brock the Badger's House

It was Christmas Eve, and Sam Pig was busy decorating the kitchen with holly. All afternoon the little pigs had been out in the woods picking bunches of holly for the great festival. They carried a heap of shining leaves and red berries home, and then they began to make the house as green as the holly bushes. Brock the Badger was away, they had not seen him for a week. He had sent a message that he would return for Christmas, and they felt sure he would come that very night. So they prepared for Christmas Day by themselves.

'Give me that big piece, Ann,' called Sam, as he balanced on top of the steps.

It was a fine piece of holly, and Sam had cut it from the high bough of a tree in the wood. With his own axe he had chopped it and he was proud of it. It was going into the chief place, on top of the shelf where Brock kept his cures and magics and spells.

Sam stretched up, but he couldn't quite reach. He tried again, and then Bill called out, 'Stand on your head, Sam.'

Sam tilted forward and fell headlong on top of his brothers and sister who were waiting below.

'Oh! Oh! Oh!' they shrieked, and there was a whirlwind of scuffling feet and wriggling tails as the four little pigs rolled over in the prickly holly on the floor.

They picked themselves up and sorted themselves out, and rubbed their bruised bodies and took the prickles from their skin.

'I couldn't help it,' cried Sam, indignantly, when Bill was angry with him. 'I didn't fall on purpose.'

'No, you fell on me,' grumbled Bill. 'Let me put it up.'

So away up the steps tripped Bill, but as he leaned over the same thing happened, and down he fell. Luckily the others had kept away and only Bill was hurt.

Then little Ann ran up the ladder, and she was so light and so nimble, she stood on tiptoes and put the holly branch on the shelf in safety.

'Oh, Sam! Sam!' she called, peering in the darkness of the magical shelf. 'I can see something up here.'

'What is it?' asked Sam.

'I don't know. Two eyes are looking at me,' said Ann.

'Nonsense, Ann. There can't be two eyes. Brock doesn't keep eyes up there. I know there's a pot of paint of all colours and a bottle of green ointment and some magical oil and a whistle that calls the wind, but there aren't any eyes.'

Ann came scurrying down. 'Yes. Two eyes, or three or four. Lots of eyes were peeping at me from behind the holly.'

'Nonsense,' said they again, rather nervously, but nobody went up the ladder. Instead they peered from the floor. They thought they saw something blink and wink, but they were not sure. They threw up a pebble and the eyes disappeared, but in a moment they were shining again from the darkness.

Sam ran to the door and looked out across the garden. The snowman was still there, shining in the pale moonlight.

'It isn't the snowman come in,' said he.

'Silly. How could he come in? He'd melt!' cried Bill.

'Never mind,' said Ann. 'Let's get on with the decorating, or Brock will come back and we shan't be ready.'

They hung up the mistletoe, and the Kissing Bunch, with its nuts and apples and a few oranges Mrs Greensleeves had given to Sam. They hung up a picture Sam had painted.

A MERRY XMAS, BROCK!

it said, in queer crooked letters. Sam read it to them, and as they couldn't read themselves they were quite happy.

They were sitting by the fire cracking nuts and popping corn when there was a thud at the door and Brock came in. He carried a sack on his back and his hat was white with snow.

'Well, little Pigs,' said he, cheerfully. 'You have made a festive room. I'm glad to get back to it. Guess where I've been!'

'To the Big House,' guessed Ann.

'To the market, Brock,' said Sam. 'Did you dare?'

'Yes, I went to the market, and walked about in the crowd and bought lots of things for our Christmas feast. I met Father Christmas, too, and he told me to say that you must not forget to hang up your stockings tonight. When I said you didn't wear stockings, he said your hats would do.'

The little Pigs ran excitedly to get the supper while Brock told his adventures. The market was bright with lamps and flares, he said. Men were shouting and pushing and nobody saw a dark Badger walking there, with his hat pulled down over his face and scarf over his nose and gloves on his furry paws. Nobody had noticed him, but a policeman had looked very hard. Luckily it was the policeman they all knew, and so he only winked and muttered: 'Goodnight. Happy Christmas, Brock.'

'I popped a Queen Elizabeth shilling in his hand for a present,' added Brock.

Then Brock spoke of the stalls with sweets and toys and turkeys and ducks.

'Wouldn't the fox like to go there!' cried Sam.

'Yes, but he daren't. He hasn't my disguise,' said Brock.

'I like a disguise,' said Sam. 'I should like to go in disguise somewhere, like the Guisers.'

They were eating their supper when there was a shuffle of feet in the snow outside and voices were heard. There was a knock. The little Pigs looked alarmed, but Brock only smiled.

'Open the door, Sam,' said he.

Sam opened a crack and looked out nervously. He saw three figures, cloaked and muffled.

'Please, Sam Pig, we are the Guisers,' said a young voice.

'We've come to sing and act our play for you, this Christmas Eve,' said a second voice in a shrill little squeak.

'Guisers,' echoed Sam, enchanted at the thought.

'Guisers,' cried Ann. 'Oh, I've always wanted to see them.'

'Come in,' called Brock, from his corner by the fire. 'Come in, Bold Guisers, and make merry.'

Indoors stepped three little animals, but nobody could see who they were. They had cloaks wrapped round them, and their faces were hidden by black masks with holes through which bright eyes peeped.

Sam glanced up to the high shelf and he could see two green eyes peering down.

'Brock! Brock!' he whispered, but Brock took no

notice. The Badger was leaning forward offering the Guisers each a mug of heather ale. They drank without moving their masks, and still no one knew who they were.

'First we'll sing a carol,' said Number One.

They sang 'The Carol of the Cherry Tree', and Sam and the others sang with them.

When they finished there was great applause, but still they kept their faces hidden.

'Now we shall give a play,' said Number One.

'It is called "The Fox and the Hen-roost",' said Number Two.

'That's an ancient play which animals have acted for a thousand years,' said Brock.

'I am the Red Hen,' squeaked a tiny voice.

'I am the Fox,' roared a deep voice.

'I am the Hen-roost and the Tree,' said the third animal. Then they acted the little play:

FOX: *'Come down, come down, my little Red Hen.*
      'Come down from yonder Tree.'

HEN: *'Oh, no! Oh, no!' said the little Red Hen.*
     'That would be the death of me.'

FOX: *'Come down, come down, my little Red Hen.*
      Come down and sup with me.'

HEN: *'Oh, no! Oh, no!' said the little Red Hen.*
     'Your supper I should be.'

FOX: *'Come down, come down, my little Red Hen.*
      Come down and marry me.'

HEN: *'Oh, no! Oh, no!' said the little Red Hen.*
       'Your bride I will never be.'
FOX: *'Come down, come down, my little Red Hen.*
       I die for love of thee.'
HEN: *'Then down I'll come,' said the little Red Hen.*
       And the Fox, he gobbled she.

The three little animals threw off their masks, and the three little pigs saw Jack Otter, Jim Otter and little Polly Otter, who lived up the river, and once had played with Sam.

They had a merry evening, telling tales, eating hot mince-pies and singing carols. Sam played his fiddle and they joined in old choruses, for the Otters knew many a ditty of the river and the water-ways which sailors sing.

Suddenly Sam remembered the eyes and he whispered to Brock. 'Someone is watching us. Someone is up on your shelf, Brock.'

Brock looked up and caught the twinkle of the little green eyes behind the holly branch.

'Come out there! I know you. Come out,' he called, and down leapt the Leprechaun.

'I came to spend Christmas with you,' cried the small fellow, dancing on the table. 'I got a ship from Ireland and I travelled with a tinker to the Christmas Fair. I crept in here, and hid on the shelf, and I was going to appear on Christmas morning, but your family spied me, Brock. You're not angry, are you, Brock? You are glad?'

'I'm delighted to welcome our old friend from Ireland to share our fun,' cried Brock. 'Father Christmas told me he had seen you. He said you'd maybe call to see us.'

The Otters were excited to talk to the Leprechaun, of whom they had heard from Sam Pig. They said they too would stay for the night, and sleep on the floor.

Ann clapped her hands when the Leprechaun made white roses blossom on the holly boughs, and nightingales sing in her work-basket. It was just like old days, she said.

'I'll make a tiny bed on the hearth for you,' she told the wee man.

'I've got the heather mattress you used to sleep on,' said Sam. 'And the pillow of wild thyme, and the blanket of wool from the black sheep,' added Tom.

'We'll feed you on honeycomb and heather ale, and mince pies and green herb cheese, and Christmas cake, and plum pudding,' said Bill.

The little Leprechaun was happy as a sand-piper, and he sat down and cobbled his shoe with a bit of bat's wing leather Brock provided.

'I must get it ready to hang up for Father Christmas,' said he. He and Brock had much to tell each other, for each was a person of great age and wisdom and knowledge of magic.

There was a gentle tap on the door, and at first nobody heard it, for everyone was laughing and talking and admiring the Leprechaun's work. The Otters were singing, the pigs were chattering, and still the tap went on.

'There's somebody else tapping beside me,' said the Leprechaun. 'Who is it?'

Sam opened the door a crack and looked out. Lady Echo stood there, in her white dress, covered with snow, and her gold hair lit up with snow-stars.

'Come in, Lady Echo,' invited Sam.

'Come in, Lady Echo,' answered the Echo, and she floated into the room, like a drift of snow. Her eyes sparkled like the stars, and a scarf blue as the sky lay on her shoulders. She was glad to be in the homely room, instead of out in the wide fields alone.

'Have you come to spend Christmas with us?' asked Sam.

'Come to spend Christmas with us,' replied the Echo, and she dropped a chaplet of snow flowers on the table and brought a little Christmas tree from the folds of her gown.

She was scarcely seated, when there was a little shrill whinny at the door, and a stamp of tiny hooves.

'Father Christmas is here,' said Sam, dashing forward to throw open the door. Nobody entered, but a flurry of snowflakes fell, smothering the floor in white. Lady Echo drew her dress close to her, the Leprechaun stopped mending his shoes, and Brock took the pipe from his mouth.

'Who's there?' he asked.

Nobody answered, but again the sharp high whinny rang through the air.

In the whiteness of the snow they could just distinguish the silvery Unicorn standing outside, with a wreath of snow on his long horn, and the silver crown on his head.

'Come in. Come in, Unicorn,' called Sam, but the Unicorn refused.

'I will stand here near your door,' said he. 'I want a word with the eight reindeer when they come with Father Christmas.'

'But you'll be so cold,' said Sam, holding out his hand.

'No, I'm in my element. I love the snow and ice,' said the little Unicorn, and he went back to the blue shadows of the snow-covered trees and waited there.

Again there was a tap at the door and this time it was a loud rap-rap-rap, which made Sam start.

'Who's that?' he called. 'Who is it?'

'It's Joe Scarecrow,' replied a high windy voice, and there on the doorstep stood the man of straw and wood, with his battered hat on his head, his wooden arms outstretched and his one leg stamping in the cold.

'Please, Master Brock,' said the scarecrow. 'I've come to wish you a Happy Christmas and many of them. When it comes, that is.'

'Come in, Joe Scarecrow,' called Brock, and the scarecrow hopped into the room and stood against the wall.

'Welcome, Joe,' said Sam.

'Spend Christmas Eve with us, Joe,' said Brock. 'We are having a party tonight. Stay the night here.'

'Thank you, Master Brock, I don't mind if I do,' said Joe .'It's main cold and sharp out in that plough-field. Nips your fingers, it does. Usually I'm taken into the barn for the winter, but Master Greensleeves has forgot me this time. I'd be glad of a bit of comfort and a sight of Christmas cheer.'

He looked round and bowed to Lady Echo, and

stared at the Leprechaun, and nodded and smiled at the company.

'You've got some grand folk here tonight. It's a bit of a do, like,' said Joe, amiably, and he removed his hat and put it on the floor.

Sam brought some sandwiches to his friend of the ploughland, and Brock gave him a mug of heather ale and Ann fetched the largest mince-pie from the oven.

'Thank ye kindly,' said Joe Scarecrow, pulling his forelock of straw, and holding up his mug to drink their healths.

Then Sam got out his fiddle, and they all sang, 'Here's a Health Unto His Majesty' and 'Peace on Earth'.

The little pigs were yawning, the Otters were blinking their round eyes, Lady Echo was singing to herself, 'Peace. Peace, Peace on Earth'. Brock said it was time everyone went to bed.

Suddenly Lady Echo began to sing in a clear, high voice a carol she had heard long long ago, and kept in her memory. The words floated in the air, and Sam listened dreamily. Then he crept softly upstairs to bed, and he hung up his hat on the bedpost. Tom, Bill and Ann followed their brother. The little Otters curled under the table and softly snored. The Leprechaun climbed into his own tiny heather bed in the corner and hung up his shoe. Joe Scarecrow took off a ragged sock and held it out. Then he shut his eyes and fell fast asleep, standing as usual on one leg.

Brock the Badger went to the door and looked out. The Unicorn stood there, as if made of ice, under the bright stars and the motionless trees. The lovely song of Lady Echo came from the room, thin and high and unearthly, bringing its memories of a Christmas long ago.

Brock waited, leaning on the doorpost, watching the sky. Suddenly he saw Father Christmas riding there on his sleigh with the eight reindeer jingling tiny bells. Down over the tree-tops came the sparkling hoofs, down to the ground. The sleigh rocked with the load of toys, and Father Christmas climbed out, waving a hand to Brock the Badger.

'Are they all ready? Are they all asleep?' he asked, in a voice soft as the fall of snow.

'Yes, they are all ready,' answered Brock. 'All except Lady Echo. She is remembering past days.'

The Unicorn awoke and stepped daintily up to the team of reinder. He nuzzled against them and talked to them in his own language, of Iceland and Greenland and Fairyland.

'I shall go with you,' said he. 'I shall travel to that land near the moon. I am ready to go tonight.'

Father Christmas was unpacking his sleigh to find presents for the company in Brock's house. He carried odd little parcels down the chimney and dropped them in the hats, the pockets, the fur pouches of the Otters, the ragged sock of Joe Scarecrow and the tiny shoe of the Leprechaun.

He drank a mug of honey-mead with Brock and stayed by the fire, with Lady Echo singing softly, and the little Otters snoring.

'A Happy Christmas, Brock, old fellow,' said he.

'Same to you, Father Christmas,' replied Brock.

'Take care of them, Brock,' said Father Christmas.

'Yes, I'll guard them from harm,' replied Brock.

Then Father Christmas said goodnight, and left his blessings on the little house. He climbed in the sleigh, and gathered up the reins. He chirruped to the eight reindeer. Then he noticed a silver horse was in front, a horse with a slender horn in its forehead, and a crown on its head.

'A Unicorn!' cried Father Christmas. 'Now that is a surprise. Where has he come from?'

'It's our Unicorn,' answered Brock, who was watching his friend start away. 'It's Sam's Unicorn, come to join you.'

'Well, I'm glad to have him, for my reindeer want extra help with the great load they have to carry now there are so many little children in the world.'

He chirruped again, and the Unicorn tossed his head and the cavalcade started up in the air, high over the tree-tops, across the blue night sky, among the stars.

'Bless you,' said Brock, and he went indoors and sat down in his big chair to sleep, but Lady Echo still sang her gentle carol: 'Peace. Peace. Peace on Earth.'

The next day Sam sprang from his bed and looked in his hat. It was bulging strangely, and he brought out a pair of bone skates.

'Happy Christmas, everybody,' he called, and all the rest awoke and felt in their hats, their socks, their purses, and their pockets.

Tom found a cookery book, and Bill found some toffee apples. Little Ann had a pair of fur mittens, and the Leprechaun found a *History of Merlin the Magician* tucked in his shoe. The little Otters had marbles made of moonstones and opals in their pockets to play with on the sandy river-bed. Joe the Scarecrow found a muffler and a stick of his favourite Blackpool rock. Lady Echo had a gleaming necklace, made of snow-pearls, and Brock the Badger felt in his furry pocket and brought out a telescope to look at the sky.

'The loveliest presents ever known in Brock the Badger's house,' cried Sam, and he ran out-of-doors to discover the marks of the reindeers' hooves and the imprints of the runners of the sleigh. The hoof marks were clear in the smooth snow, with the little Unicorn's dainty prints.

On the snow lay a little silver circle, the crown the Unicorn had worn. It had fallen off when he rose in the sky with Father Christmas.

Sam took it to Brock, who hung it on the Christmas Tree.

They stood round and held hands, and sang the

Christmas Day hymn for all things, great and small, men and children and animals.

'A Happy Christmas, World. A Happy Christmas, World,' they cried, and their small voices flew out over the hills to the stars, while down on earth the church bells rang their merry peal.

ABOUT THE AUTHOR

Alison Uttley was born in 1887 in Derbyshire, and was brought up on a farm some distance from a village, which meant she dwelt in a real solitude of fields and woods. She was never lonely – she had calves, lambs, foals, dogs, and her small brother for companions, as well as country people, the hedger, the ditcher, Irish haymakers and the oatcake man.

She won a scholarship to a small grammar school, and although her chief interest was music, she turned to mathematics and science and went to Manchester University, gaining a degree in Physics Honours. After going to Cambridge for a year, where she studied English with pleasure and surprise, she taught science at a London school, then married a civil engineer and had a son.

The child listened eagerly to her stories, which she had secretly been writing in an attic, and she finally sent one to a publisher, who made a book of it and asked for more, to her astonishment. Since then her animal characters Little Grey Rabbit, Hare, Squirrel, Sam Pig, Brock the Badger, Tim Rabbit, Brown Mouse, Little Red Fox have been compared with the creations of Beatrix Potter.

Her first book, *The Country Child*, first published in 1931, is also available in Puffins.

Mrs Uttley died in May 1976.

Some Other Young Puffins

ADVENTURES OF SAM PIG   *Alison Uttley*

Ten funny and magical stories about Alison Uttley's
best-loved creation.

MAGIC AT MIDNIGHT   *Phyllis Arkle*

Wild Duck had stood motionless on his inn sign for 200 years
or more, but the night he heard of the midnight magic he
stiffly flapped his wings and came down to try the world.

ONCE THERE WAS A BOY AND
OTHER STORIES   *Malcolm Carrick*

Once there was a boy, a girl, a postman, a king, a queen, a
shopping list, a tug-of-war, a pair of odd socks – all funny or
interesting enough to yield these enchanting stories by a new
author.

STORIES FOR FIVE-YEAR-OLDS
STORIES FOR SIX-YEAR-OLDS
STORIES FOR SEVEN-YEAR-OLDS
Sara and Stephen Corrin

Celebrated anthologies of stories specially selected for each
age group and tested in the classroom by the editors.

FANTASTIC MR FOX   *Roald Dahl*

Every evening Mr Fox would creep down into the valley in
the darkness and help himself to a nice plump chicken, duck,
or turkey, but there came a day when Farmers Boggis, Bunce
and Bean determined to stop him whatever the cost . . .

GONE IS GONE *Wanda Gag*

Farmer Fritzl thought his wife's job of keeping house was
easy, so he stayed home to try it. But the bad dog, the naughty
baby and the cow that fell off the roof soon made him change
his mind.

THE SHRINKING OF TREEHORN
Florence Parry Heide

'Nobody shrinks,' declared Treehorn's father, but Treehorn
was shrinking, and it wasn't long before even the unshakeable
adults had to admit it.

ALL ABOUT THE BULLERBY CHILDREN
Astrid Lindgren

Delightful stories about the six children who live side by
side in the Swedish village of Bullerby, and about their
family celebrations and adventures.

THE BUS UNDER THE LEAVES *Margaret Mahy*

Adam didn't even like David, until they began playing in the
old bus that made such a wonderful hideout, and soon they
were the best of friends.

BANDICOOT AND HIS FRIENDS *Violet Philpott*

Lion promised his friends a surprise when he came home
from India, but no one expected anything half as nice as
friendly, funny, furry, little Bandicoot, who was so kind and
clever when any of his friends were in trouble.

PLEASANT FIELDMOUSE *Jan Wahl*

'I am a Fireman,' Pleasant Fieldmouse painted outside his
house, but he was also a picnic organizer, a rose grower, a
rescuer of captured ladies, and a brave and cheerful character
as well.

If you have enjoyed reading this book and would like to know about others which we publish, why not join the Puffin Club? You will be sent the club magazine, *Puffin Post*, four times a year and a smart badge and membership book. You will also be able to enter all the competitions. For details of cost and an application form, send a stamped addressed envelope to:

The Puffin Club Dept A
Penguin Books Limited
Bath Road
Harmondsworth
Middlesex